3/2000

DEATH AND DECEPTION

DEATH AND DECEPTION

•

CAT LYONS

AVALON BOOKS
THOMAS BOUREGY AND COMPANY, INC.
401 LAFAYETTE STREET
NEW YORK, NEW YORK 10003

© Copyright 1998 by Cat Lyons
Library of Congress Catalog Card Number: 98-96618
ISBN 0-8034-9329-0
All rights reserved.
All the characters in this book are fictitious,
and any resemblance to actual persons,
living or dead, is purely coincidental.

PRINTED IN THE UNITED STATES OF AMERICA
ON ACID-FREE PAPER
BY HADDON CRAFTSMEN, BLOOMSBURG, PENNSYLVANIA

For Tristan and Ben

Chapter One

"I don't know—" The old woman caught her breath; her eyes widened then suddenly narrowed. When she spoke again her voice quavered, becoming harsh and sour. "I don't know any Madeline Paige."

Madeline was stunned. Having identified herself, she'd expected the cool, damp veranda to instantly become a warm, cozy place. She had envisioned the older woman throwing open the door, grabbing and hugging her, smiling, choking with long-felt sorrow, eyes flooding with fresh happiness—everything warm and wonderful. But that wasn't happening; there was only silence—shocked, furious silence. She wasn't wanted. Madeline fought off the exploding realization, barricading her mind against the terrible thought. She sought other explanations but it was futile—she wasn't wanted, never was. The simmering excitement that had been growing inside her, building for days, suddenly became cold and black and hollow.

Eye to eye, inches apart from Madeline, the woman's eyes had grown small and hard; she was glaring. Madeline couldn't move. She couldn't think or breathe. She didn't understand. Shrinking back, she managed to look away, down at her shoes and the dust, and the gray chipped paint. This couldn't be real, it couldn't be happening, not like this. Risking a fresh glance up, she caught the swing of the heavy oak door, the *kathunk* as it closed with grim finality. "You can't," she gasped, before adding in a whisper, "please, you can't just . . ."

Anne Shannon was gone. The brief meeting was over, over so quick it was like it had never happened.

Madeline remained on the veranda. She still clutched the wooden edge of the open screen door. The woman was not at all what she had expected. A thought welled up inside her; it couldn't be resisted: the woman was horrid. The black eyes, eyes that at first seemed so dull and vacant and then flashed with cold animosity—could it possibly have been hatred?—at the mention of the name Madeline Paige. It was the name that caused the eruption of rage, the snarky "I don't know any Madeline Paige." But she did know—she lied, she must have lied. You could hear the sudden change in the woman's voice. Anne Shannon knew the name, and that's why she reacted so abruptly and sourly. Of course, how could she not know Madeline Paige?

But worse than that, Madeline disliked the older woman instantly. She made her knees quiver and her heart buckle. She was scared of her. Why did the woman look so old? Madeline hadn't expected that—the short, stringy gray hair, the sallow skin. She wasn't that old; she shouldn't look so old.

Madeline struggled with an urge to flee. But I can't leave. What can I do? I can't just stand here; I couldn't possibly knock again.

The thought of not liking, of not loving, her mother had never occurred to Madeline. The mother in the book was warm and joyous, sweet, laughing, kind, tender, wonderful—how could this be the same woman? How could this be happening? Never had Madeline considered she might not like her mother, her own mother. It wasn't possible.

The house was quiet. The world was still, the air so moist and heavy it threatened to suffocate her like a thick cloak. Alone on the veranda, Madeline was three thousand miles from home and feeling tired, hurt, and foolish, and more desolate than ever before. Dumbstruck, she kept waiting, shivering, desperate to escape but refusing to budge, torn between pounding on the door and crying. Could she run all the way back home? Taxi to the little bus station in Saint Andrews, then to Saint John, to Montreal, to California, more long flights, and bus rides, and taxis. And yet she couldn't stay here or knock on that door again. Had she set out on this long trek for a mere thirty seconds of terror and rudeness from her mother? After twenty years?

Madeline's trembling hand found the paperback in her jacket pocket and squeezed it. There was so much love on those pages; that's what made it special—warm love—but here . . .

Taking one step back, she faltered, not wanting to leave but terrified of lingering only to be confronted by that woman again. Tears were beginning to well in her eyes. With a shiver Madeline backed off the veranda. Nearly stumbling down the wooden steps, she ran across the deep grass, dew licking at her corduroy slacks and cotton canvas shoes.

She'd been naive. A woman who could abandon her own infant daughter would not joyously embrace a surprise reunion. For the last few days, since she had discovered the book, she'd been too excited to stop and think. On the gravel lane Madeline walked quickly, head down, numb. Still her mind spun. She should never have come. She should have written first, or phoned. What had she been thinking?

Yet how could a woman reject outright her own flesh and blood—her own daughter? Had she no heart? There was compassion in the book, great love between the mother and daughter; they'd been buddies, integral halves of an inseparable team. How was it possible? And yet years ago Anne Shannon must have created an elaborate ruse to desert her teammate, her young child. Why?

Safely hidden away in the murky shadows of tall trees, Madeline glanced back at the cottage. It was small, built of gray limestone blocks, old and sedate, with two dormers thrusting forward out of the green shingles. A wide veranda and white railing encircled the building. Lacy white gingerbread adorned the overhangs, and ivy coated one wall and grew up thick and robust on the chimney. The cottage looked out upon the bay; she could smell the sea close by, still hidden in the early morning mist.

A curtain shifting in an upstairs window startled her and Madeline backed away. Suddenly she wanted to hurry.

Chapter Two

Across the lobby a door bounced open. Before her a young man appeared with his back to her but he hastily swung around. Looking up, he saw Madeline and faltered slightly. Three breakfast plates were balanced flat along his left arm. The plates wobbled. They began to escape his grasp, sliding away. He rushed to steady them with his right hand, though it too was encumbered with four slender vases filled with pink and white flowers.

Tall and slim, he had easy blue eyes that flashed with casual alarm, but when Madeline lunged forward and rescued two plates from him, he smiled amiably. Those marvelous, happy blue eyes sought and caught and pierced her own. For an instant he paused, then as he took back the plates he announced with abundant relief, "Am I glad to see you. Thank goodness you're early."

Madeline felt his eyes dally upon her, like a slow tickle; she shrank back.

He saw her discomfort. He turned away saying, "Wait just a sec." The hardwood floors squeaked with each step as he left her.

She watched him go beyond the front desk, through the lobby, into the dining area. Madeline was breathing fast and part of her mind still lingered on the veranda of the old stone cottage. *"Thank goodness you're early?"* she wondered, the words slowly sinking in. *Early for what?* Wasn't the restaurant open? She could see guests eating, one couple anyway—a gentleman, rock-bald with a trim mustache, and a woman with tightly curled gray hair. The table they shared was out on the porch, up against wide windows. Madeline looked away when the man glanced toward her.

Throughout the small inn there was a glow of warm wood: the floor, front desk, armchairs and side tables, a hutch, and even the moldings and the eye-level plate rack that held dishes, vases, and small figurines were all gleaming honey-colored wood. The last of a fire flickered in the open fireplace. She stood near the hearth and reached out her hands, seeking the comforting heat.

"Okay." The young man was back beside her but in a hurry and he only slowed long enough to take her hand. "I'm Steven. Let's get started, shall we?" Off again, he pushed through the swinging doors, obviously expecting her to follow. Madeline hesitated. He was leading her away from the dining area, away from the tables and chairs, away from where people sat and ate and rested and enjoyed the peaceful ambience; instead he was taking her into a back room.

Madeline had just happened upon the Harbourview Inn as she trudged back toward Saint Andrew's-by-the-Sea. The thought of a soothing cup of hot coffee and a chance to sit a moment and collect her thoughts drew her past the hedge, the white gate, and up the limestone path through a corner of dew-drenched English garden to the old and pretty inn.

She found herself following him: nudging open the swinging door, leaning into a bright kitchen, into a warm bastion of rich fragrances. Her stomach took note and growled with anticipation.

The kitchen was long and narrow with stoves and ovens and counters occupying most of the perimeter. A stainless steel island ran down the middle. Every surface was cluttered—mixing bowls, measuring cups, knives, spoons, food processors, cutting boards, canisters of flour and sugar, eggshells, onion skins.... Already Steven was busy massaging a sheet of pastry with a rolling pin. "So, what do you like to do?"

Madeline was becoming very hungry. Staring, unable to think, she hesitated. Why did he ask such a

Death and Deception

question? "I like . . ." But he was irresistibly friendly; his eyes were especially exhilarating. ". . . to eat."

Steven erupted with an easy laughter; it took a moment before he managed to utter, "That's good."

Had she said something funny? She had come into this quaint little spot to have something to eat; wasn't that what people did? She was becoming ravenous.

"Well, I hate to start you peeling potatoes"—he nodded toward a huge burlap sack propped up in the corner—"what drudgery, but I'm in the middle of rolling out this pastry." He dusted a little flour on the rolling pin and kept speaking briskly. "The agency told you this position wasn't just for a waitress, right? That it's also kitchen help and, well, any old thing really, a lot of odd jobs?"

It was a question, Madeline realized. "But—" She missed her chance to protest.

"Don't worry." He recognized her concern. "Just be a bit flexible, try your best, that's all I ask. If you don't like peeling potatoes, maybe we can—"

Beyond the door a bell tinkled.

"The O'Dwyers." A kettle began to chug steam and tried to whistle. "Must want a fresh pot of tea." He was nodding to the struggling kettle and wiping his hands.

Behind him a phone rang. Steven wavered, torn between getting the kettle or the phone. On the shelf above the center island a white plastic timer began to ding. There was a long row of little timers, many of them merrily clicking away. With a small grin he rolled his eyes and asked, "Can you?" He nodded again toward the kettle. It was right there on the stove, close beside her, steaming, waiting. Madeline turned slightly.

"Your knapsack and windbreaker can go there on the hooks by the top of the stairs." He was reaching for the phone. "You're a lifesaver." His smile was infectious; somehow Madeline found she too was beginning to forget, beginning to smile a little.

He had the phone snagged in the crook of his neck and he said hello while walking over to the still-ringing timer; he hit the top and the irritating noise stopped. Glancing at a sheet of paper beneath the timer, he kept speaking into the phone while he looked at the ovens directly behind him.

The kettle's whistle was becoming shrill and insistent. There were teapots stationed conveniently on the shelf above. He had mistaken her for someone else, she realized, and in a moment she would explain, but in the meantime surely she could help out and make one pot of tea. At least that would shut up the screaming kettle. Madeline shrugged out of her knapsack and coat.

She heard him announce, "They've added another twenty-two guests. I know! Of course they won't fit in the chapel, never would. Well, for dinner we can spread into the lobby easily enough, but we need to find some more tables and we're short eighteen chairs.

I figure we'll have to drag in some of the garden furniture.'' Moving over to the oven, he dropped down the door and threw a questioning glance back at Madeline. She took the kettle off the burner.

With a bunched-up tea towel Steven drew a cookie sheet out of the oven, grimacing, and murmured, "Ah, ow, ow—hot!" The tin sheet clattered onto the counter as golden croissants jounced lightly into the air. He flapped his hands and blew at his fingertips, still able to intersperse the mumbled words, "I know, Mom, oven mitts." He was reaching back into the oven, pulling out more croissants, still not wearing any oven mitts. "Really? But aren't they the competition?"

Madeline caught his eyes. She held up the teapot and shrugged.

Steven displayed three fingers. "They'll just loan us the tables?" He spoke into the phone as he moved toward her, the cluttered stainless-steel counter between them. On the top shelf where the teapot was, he nudged forward a cardboard box filled with tea bags. He announced "Great" into the phone as he bent over the croissants and stared, then jabbed one with his finger. It didn't explode or crumble and he seemed happy with that, so he tore off a flaky tip, and cautiously tasted it.

Madeline poured steaming water into the pot, drowning three tea bags. *Now what?* she wondered. There was a faint tinkle again. The guests were calling.

Steven, phone still locked in the crook of his neck, reached over the counter and dangled a morsel of croissant close up before her. His eyes questioned. She responded by opening her mouth and reaching out with her teeth; she drew the bread from his fingertips: rich, hot, exquisite. It melted on contact with her tongue. Her countenance must have reflected her rapture, because Steven's eyes sparkled with delight. He pushed a wicker basket across the counter. In it there was a slate-blue napkin cradling four more steaming croissants.

Another timer went off as Madeline backed through the swinging doors, teapot in one hand, wicker basket in the other. He was still on the phone; she heard him say before the doors closed, "Okay, I've got all that." His voice slipped lower and slowed. "So, what's the latest on Dad?" The door swung shut.

Expectant faces turned toward her as she crossed the lobby and approached the table. Without preparation, a stream of words began to flow out almost naturally. "Sorry to keep you waiting," Madeline said softly. "More tea?" She shifted the thin white vase with small pink carnations and sprigs of baby's breath to the end of the table against the window and centered the basket.

The gentleman wore a tweed sports jacket. He was tall and gaunt, smooth, self-satisfied. He smiled effusively as he peeled back the napkin. A wisp of steam escaped. Mrs. O'Dwyer sat across from her husband.

Death and Deception 13

She was small, tanned, and impeccably dressed in a camel-colored jacket, a light turtleneck sweater, and black slacks. "Oh my, how can we keep eating?"

"How can we not?" Mr. O'Dwyer countered, as he snatched up a hot croissant.

It appeared they expected Madeline to clear away dirty dishes, so she took up the empty teapot and two plates dabbed with egg smudges, scattered crumbs, and slivers of orange rind and kiwi peel.

The gentleman grinned, speaking as he chewed. "You see, what did I tell you, here comes the sun." Sure enough the sun was beginning to burn through the heavy morning mist. Beyond the wall of windows the veil was being drawn back from the lovely garden. In the distance a small corner of the wide bay was visible, silver and shimmering. "Going to be a splendid day for a wedding," he went on.

"Yes. Provided young Stevie can handle it."

The gentleman scoffed, then continued on in a fine, deep, and melodious voice, "Of course, he can. He's doing a marvelous thing leaping into the fray like this. Parents must be awfully proud, awfully. A fine lad."

"I never said he wasn't, but—" The woman frowned. She was a bubbling stew of worries and she resented her husband's glee and childish, last-day-of-school attitude. A wedding was serious business. "I don't see how he can manage a wedding reception all by himself, I really don't."

The gentleman nodded toward Madeline as she retreated. "He's not alone." Madeline glanced back, and immediately a fork slid off the plates and clattered to the floor.

"Besides, a mishap or two adds a dash of color to the memories, eh?" Then he added with enthusiasm—evidently he delighted in teasing his wife—"Just remember our wedding?" He cupped his wife's small hand beneath his.

"Yes, well, it's certainly something I've tried hard to forget. Flat tire? I'd've never believed it."

Madeline glanced back as O'Dwyer shrugged and smirked. Briskly snatching up the fork, she hurried away into the lobby. Across from the front desk, near the fireplace, a young woman had come in. She waited, warming herself before the fading embers. Her full apple cheeks shone even rosier because of her starch-white skin. She was young, short, and plump, with large, gentle doelike eyes and dark hair drawn back in a thick French braid. The girl stared at Madeline, wide-eyed and hopeful.

"Umm, hi," Madeline stammered. "Have a seat. Can I get you a cup of tea, or coffee?"

At first the girl was tongue-tied, then finally she whispered in a shy, high-pitched, shivering voice, "Oh, tea would be very nice. Please and thank you."

Over Madeline's shoulder a family of four was descending the staircase from the rooms above. "Coffee, when you get a chance," the man called, "and those famous croissants. I could smell them, warm and wonderful, so we rushed on down.''

Madeline returned his smile, then escaped back to the relative sanctuary of the kitchen. Without thinking, she had allowed herself to be swept up into the happy cocoon of Steven's chaotic life. Slender as a blade of grass, nevertheless she felt bull-like energy pulsing within, energy born of frustration and confusion. Yet she didn't want to think about her mother; she wasn't ready. The best tonic for anxiety was hard work; instinctively, she craved hectic hard work, till her mind could fall blank, till her muscles ached, until she was so bone weary she could sleep like a stone and forget, at least for a little while. The wound was fresh, tender, and very deep. It was best to set it aside for now, let time create distance and begin the healing process.

Back in the kitchen Steven was still on the phone. "Yes, she's here already; the agency could only send one. Hey, tell me about it.... I know, I've already spoken to Diane, yes, and begged Lois.... Yes, reluctantly. We'll manage fine, don't worry." He was wrapping up small cubes of braised and marinated meat in thin pastry. He pinched along the seams and arranged them on cookie sheets; they looked like rows of tiny presents.

Another bag of Earl Grey tea went into a small china teapot and steaming water was added. Madeline saw the big coffee urn. The red light was on, so she grabbed a carafe and toggled the lever.

"Phone again in about an hour. I'm sure I'll have more questions by then," he added with a chuckle, striving to be upbeat but belying some concern. "Yes, I better. Okay, let me know, and you're sure we've got to go with those smoked scallops?" Steven laughed; he was stretching out the phone cord as he moved over to the big steel sinks. Then he said goodbye.

"More customers," Madeline announced. She had the pot of coffee and the tea and pushed back out to the lobby.

Steven finished washing his hands, drying them quickly, then he ran after her, hanging up the phone as he passed and picking up more flower vases and baskets of croissants. From close behind, as they passed through the swinging door, he whispered, "You wouldn't happen to know anything about smoking scallops, would you?"

Blankly, Madeline responded, "Scallops? A kind of creamy potato thing, right?"

"Great," he said, drawing out the word long and slow.

Madeline ignored his response because as she approached the dining area, many more faces turned to her expectantly. The scent of fresh coffee and croissants had filtered through the rambling old country inn and drawn all the guests out from the woodwork. "Do you have menus?" she murmured. "How does it work?" She had no experience with this kind of thing.

Death and Deception

Handing out pots of tea was one thing, but waiting tables—well, she really hadn't a clue what to do. She was beginning to panic. Didn't she need a pen and a little pad? She wouldn't be able to remember everything.

There it was again: his easy, confident eyes spoke directly to her soul, the infectious smile made her respond in kind.

"I'll handle this for now," he said. "You're a lifesaver. Thanks, Jessica."

"Jessica?" Madeline questioned. "I'm not Jessica."

"But the agency—"

"I, I . . ." The young girl with the long braid shifted in her chair. She'd been watching them intently. Looking about herself, she started to stand. "I'm Jessica."

Another couple had come down the stairs. They passed behind, chanting to all, "Good morning." Immediately the room became a hubbub of lively chatter: from the weather, the croissants, the kippers and eggs, the bride, the dress, the big white peonies, to "Have you seen the darling little chapel in the woods?"

Steven whispered, "Then who are you?"

She held out her hand. "Madeline Rosetti."

"Steven Raven." They shook again. "But . . ."

Jessica waited.

"Um—" Steven hesitated. "I'm sorry, I thought—"

"It's okay, it was fun while it lasted. I just came in

for a cup of coffee." She felt her spirits sinking. "And if you can spare one of those fabulous croissants..."

"Sure." Steven was struggling. He was captivated. She was so very pretty. Her subtlest movement, any movement at all, enraptured him, held him spellbound and electrically charged; it was like a lone feather was loose and dancing along his spine. Guests waited impatiently; a dozen enterprises were on the go in the kitchen; the new girl, Jessica, looked hopelessly lost; but above all, he knew he didn't want to let Madeline leave. The family with the two young children were looking hungrily at the baskets of croissants that Steven still carried. Outside, a truck shifted gears as the motor labored up the slight rise to the front of the inn. Another timer went off in the kitchen; you could just hear the alarm calling.

Steven tried to smile. He was torn, trying to move in several directions at once. "Jessica," he started, "could you..." He handed her the croissants.

Jessica stood with a blank, almost frightened expression. Reluctantly, she raised her hands and accepted the wicker baskets, but remained stationary, waiting for more instructions.

For Madeline the charade was over. It had been kind of fun while it lasted but now it was time to move on. Where to, Madeline didn't exactly know. She could feel the disappointment in Steven's eyes; he wanted her to stay. It sounded like he could use all the help he could get.

Death and Deception

The phone kept ringing. There was a friendly *toot-toot* from the truck horn.

Impulsively, Madeline shrugged and blurted out, "Okay, we'll get these folks some tea, or coffee." Then she added hastily, for the benefit of the eyes upon her, "and lots of croissants for everyone. I take it Jessica is new?" Madeline was beginning to feel like an old hand.

Steven nodded with relief. Coming back to life, he started to hurry into the kitchen, then slowed long enough to call back, "Thanks, and they'll probably want eggs, just find out what style, and orange juice too. And you're getting way behind with those potatoes."

"Scalloped, right?" she questioned, then threw him a good-natured scowl; it caused him to begin to laugh just as he disappeared.

A moment later the phone stopped ringing, beneath the building a garage door clattered open, then Steven was running back into the kitchen and turning off a noisy timer and reaching for an oven door. He muttered with disgust, "Great. Soft-boiled egg, and dry toast. On a diet, she wants a soft-boiled egg and dry toast. I can't do soft-boiled eggs! And now everyone will see the"—his voice went squeaky, but his eyes were still jovial—"precious little egg cups. Now everyone will want one to play with. And there will be a flood of requests for soft-boiled eggs, and they'll be too runny or too hard."

Madeline filled a carafe with coffee and asked, "You do the world's best croissants but you can't soft-boil an egg?"

"They never turn out for me. The croissants I've practiced like you wouldn't believe. There are stacks of rejects out in the compost pile."

Madeline chuckled. Soft-boiled eggs had been her standard breakfast for years. "Okay, I'll do your eggs for you, if you'll do some . . . kipper things, for that big fellow in the back corner. What *are* kippers, anyway?"

"Salty, smelly fish, sort of good though," Steven answered. "And you had better make at least six of those eggs."

"Why?"

His answer was to grab a wicker basket from the top shelf. Inside there were small, ornate egg cups, made of porcelain and beautifully hand-painted, with lids! Steven chose one and pulled back the top. It sang, or at least tinkled, a little tune. The one he had opened played "Lara's Theme."

Madeline grinned with delight. She removed another lid. This one played "Greensleeves."

"I see what you mean," she said, and she added five more large brown eggs to the water.

Chapter Three

During the morning Madeline caught herself laughing and enjoying herself. Peeling potatoes, dicing onions, washing dishes, mopping hardwood floors, clearing and setting tables, hopping to the whims of guests and the incessant demands of little plastic timers—she delighted in the work. She was solving problems, gaining a sense of accomplishment, and above all she found the strong, convivial, irrepressible presence of Steven exhilarating. There were moments when she completely forgot about the past and Anne Shannon, about her California home, and the future, and she forgot about the book that brought her here; instead she found herself working on her chores, watching and wondering about Steven Raven.

Madeline looked down at the paper once more.

From the enormous alphabetized rack running along the side wall she took out jars of rosemary and marjoram, measured and sprinkled some of each on the chopped vegetables, stirred in chunks of fresh garlic and olive oil, then she placed the lid on top and carried the roasting pan into the walk-in refrigerator. Another task was complete; now, for the first time in hours, she felt the lack of a pressing chore nipping at her ankles.

In a corner of the kitchen Jessica had collapsed. She wilted at the little table by the side window overlooking the herb garden. Her head drooped down to the tabletop and nestled into the crux of her arms. She inhaled deeply, her eyes fell shut, and slowly she exhaled.

"Looks like it must be break time," Steven announced. He replaced a clipboard on a wall hook, then added, "Thanks to you two wonder workers, we're pretty well all caught up."

Madeline eyed the vacant chair across from Jessica. Her lower back ached; she was tired; rest beckoned. She had originally only come into the little inn to sit down, relax, and clear her mind. This was her chance. It was quiet and peaceful now; the inn was temporarily empty. Soon the crowd would return and the wedding reception would begin; she knew it would be pandemonium.

Steven moved past her and Jessica. He started to open the back door, slowed, turned, and mentioned,

"I'm going down to the chapel, just to check on how things are coming along."

It was all the invitation Madeline needed. Steven had become her security blanket. When he was near, when she could see him, she felt relaxed and happy. He had that effect. But when he was gone, even if only for a few moments, she felt anxious and alone.

"How long have you been doing this?" Madeline asked as she followed him outside.

"In earnest, only about two, three weeks," he answered. He was leading her through the kitchen garden. There were tomato plants on one side, thick tall bean vines on the other. "I'm just filling in for my parents. My father is ill and my mother doesn't want to leave him. He's in a hospital in Toronto."

She could tell by the way that he spoke and the shadow that crept into his expressive eyes that the illness was serious, and that he loved his father very much. "I'm sorry to hear that."

Steven nodded. "I teach at a small college in Ottawa, and, unlike my sisters, I have most of the summer free, so I sometimes help out a bit doing odd jobs. This time I got appointed emergency fill-in innkeeper." With a father seriously ill, it sounded like he too was submerging his troubles in hard work. "Luckily, my mother is a compulsive organizer. She writes down her recipes and in fact every procedure, step by step, so I'm managing okay. Tonight might be a bit of a challenge though."

At the end of the garden he reached back and took her hand and led Madeline along a thin path through the tall grass. Brushing aside a swooping low pine bough, they slipped into a small copse of trees. They were alone in the dark cool shadows. He still held her hand; he did it so naturally it was like he wasn't even aware of it, but Madeline was. Ahead the shadows ended. There was a meadow. Madeline could see soft light and scattered patches of brilliant color: bearded irises, white daisies, dandelions and faded daffodils, tall orange lilies haphazardly strewn on a bed of green. The light—filtered by haze and trees and leaves, the dark tree shadows and daubs of vibrant color—combined like a painting by Renoir, only it was real, and smelled real and wonderfully fresh. In the center of the meadow there was a cabin with a small spire. There were young children everywhere. Someone tossed a peewee football up into the air and a pack of kids chased after it. Uncomfortable shoes, jackets, and ties were discarded and used for field markers. Shirttails flapped as the boys ran. A few young girls, restrained by a greater sense of decorum, not to mention hard shoes and pretty summer dresses, congregated by the lane not far from the chapel's front steps where an open carriage, a driver, and a chestnut mare waited to trot the newlyweds away.

Steven looked at his watch. He scanned across the meadow. "Jeremy," he called out, trying to be heard but not too loud at the same time.

In the field one of the younger boys stopped running. He glanced at Steven, looked back at the game, then reluctantly bounded through the grass. He had wild hair and red flushed cheeks.

"How's the wedding going?" Steven asked as the boy drew close.

Jeremy shrugged, gasping for air. "It's too little," he said, referring to the chapel. "The kids don't fit in."

Steven nodded. "But have you seen a wedding before?" Even speaking with a small child, Steven's voice had the same friendly timbre Madeline noticed he used with everyone: guest, hired help, mother, and child alike.

The boy shrugged again. He couldn't recall if he had or not.

"Have they exchanged rings yet?"

Jeremy didn't understand why this should be of any interest to him.

"You do still have the rings, I hope?"

The boy stopped in confusion and looked up at Steven. He grabbed into his pockets. Suddenly a look of panic swept over him; his hands squirreled around deeper in his pockets, then he gasped and breathed again.

As the boy sped off, Steven stated calmly, with a late-blooming smile, "The ring bearer."

"He isn't wearing any shoes," Madeline noted.

"No. Or socks," Steven added with a laugh. "Or his jacket and tie, but luckily he still has the rings."

The boy reached the door just as his mother appeared. With exasperation she hauled him into the chapel, tucking in his shirt and smoothing his hair as they went. A ripple of laughter filtered out of the little building.

Built over a hundred years ago from hand-hewn birch logs chinked with white plaster, the chapel had only improved with the passage of time. The inside wood sparkled. No cars were visible—everyone had parked at the inn or the nearby cottages and taken the gravel lane or the path behind the inn through the trees. Only one other building was visible, and even then it was just the corner of a green shingle roof that peeked out beyond a veil of dark, trembling leaves—a dormer, with a hint of lacy white gingerbread. Recognizing Anne Shannon's cottage caught Madeline's attention and revived the tightness in her throat.

Curiosity, tweaked by their friend being called away, drew all the children in close. A hush descended as they huddled around the chapel windows and doors. Madeline and Steven stood at the rear and watched. She recognized the O'Dwyers and several other guests from breakfast. The groom's hands fumbled with the wedding band as he tried to pick it up. He glanced at his bride to see if she had noticed. Madeline knew their eyes had met. Now the groom relaxed and he took firm hold, and he smiled as he slipped the ring onto the bride's delicate white finger.

Barefoot, Jeremy stood in the aisle; beside him, a tiny flower girl waited, motionless, like a china doll in flowing satin, white gloves, and even wearing shoes.

The crowd pressed in tighter. Madeline fit snug and warm, pushed back, almost against Steven's chest. She watched the groom lift the bride's thin veil; he waited a moment, then the bride smiled. Shyly they kissed. The hushed silence broke with whispers and a smattering of applause.

Steven found Madeline's hand and took it up in his own. He slipped out of the crowd and led her away. He continued to hold her hand as they crossed the fields in the tall grass and the wildflowers.

She was feeling trembly and annoyed with herself. Good-looking, self-confident men intimidated her; she knew that. But all day she had seen things in Steven's eyes that couldn't be there. She hardly knew him, not at all. What with her traumatic meeting with her mother, her long travels and tiring morning, she knew she'd been disarmed by her heightened emotional state. She was imagining things. Everything today was conspiring to wrest away the rigid control she always maintained over her life.

As they approached the back door Steven caught her eyes and murmured, "Battle stations." He released her hand as he opened the door for her. "The potatoes have to go in the oven. And don't forget to set the timer. And the scallops, you've got that under control, right?"

Without missing a beat, Madeline snapped back, "Of course. Jessica said it's some kind of lumpy seafood thing, right?"

Jessica heard her name. She looked up and opened her eyes. She tried to smile as she shambled to her feet.

Chapter Four

Every muscle was a flickering ribbon of tingling ache; it felt good. Madeline luxuriated in her fatigue. The inn was quiet; the last of the dishes were almost done. Madeline's hands kept scouring round and round, back and forth, her eyes becoming glassy. The crud on the big roasting pans was impervious to her scrubbing. She kept working. Her mind began to roam; she was too tired to maintain control.

Thoughts of her mother were beginning to resurface with frightening regularity. *"I don't know any Madeline Paige."* She kept scrubbing. She kept seeing those black eyes, hearing the harsh voice, and then there was the letter. That letter had shattered any possible hope that could have remained. She knew it at the time, but hadn't allowed herself the moment to consider it. She wasn't wanted. Her mother hated her. In her back pocket Madeline could feel the stiff crispness of the envelope. During the frenzy of preparing the scallops, Steven had handed her the letter, just a note, really. He had found it lying on the front desk, and she could see in his eyes he was curious—who would leave her a letter at the front desk? Why hadn't they just asked to speak to her? Who knew her, who knew she was here?

Madeline was curious too. She first thought it was some sort of mistake. She only knew two people here, Steven and Anne. But there was no mistake. The note only took a second to read. *Go away. Leave. Leave now. There is nothing here for you.* Clear, concise, unequivocal. Not a threat exactly, but certainly not a welcome, and there was no doubt where it had come from. Anne Shannon was not about to have a change of heart; she didn't want to see Madeline again. If the person you had traveled thousands of miles to see could only say "Go away," and slam the door in your face, then what was the point of staying?

Madeline decided it was time. Abandoning the big roasting pans to soak overnight in the soapy water, she slipped off her white apron and dried her hands, then dropped it down the laundry chute.

The small inn was quiet once again; only the grandfather clock ticked away, faintly, like a sleeper's heartbeat. The evening had flown by in circuslike pandemonium. Steven had been ringmaster, featured acrobat, clown, and tightrope walker; he even cleaned up after the elephants.

She collected her coat and knapsack. In the lobby, Madeline saw a broom in the archway leading to the dining porch. The reflection of one lit candle flickered in the window. Steven was sitting in a corner, feet splayed apart propped up on another chair, head back, eyes half shut, a snifter of cognac cupped in his hands and resting on his lap. The easy smile was worn down and yet more content than ever. Suspicious that he was no longer alone, the eyes opened; his head bobbed up as he swung around. "Oh, thank goodness it's only you."

"Only?"

"Sorry." Even now his eyes managed a sparkle. "You know what I mean. I'm just glad it isn't some inebriated sod desiring another drink or eager to dance one more Hokey Pokey."

"So you don't want to give me a drink, and you don't want to dance with me?"

He grinned. "I'd love to, but I don't believe I have the energy even to fall out of this chair. But there is cognac here if you'd like, and if you are still feeling peppy, I'd be glad to watch you dance." He offered her his snifter. "But you must be exhausted too."

With tired sarcasm she answered, "No, not at all."

He expended the energy for one more smile. "Why not relax a bit and join me?"

Madeline sank into the seat at his side, sitting for

the first time since she had arrived at the inn that morning. She leaned back and put her feet on the seat opposite.

Steven said softly, as he offered her the glass, "I don't know what I would have done without you." There was a bond between them forged from the camaraderie of hard work and success, for the evening had been a roaring triumph.

She brought the fat glass to her lips, closed her eyes, took a tiny sip, and allowed the fire to loll about her tongue.

"You're tired," he announced.

Madeline nodded, eyes still closed. She swallowed.

"Me too, but I know I won't be able to sleep for a while. I'm too keyed up. I don't know how we pulled it off. Things kept going wrong...." A new thought occurred to him. "Like the wine. The cases said red but inside the bottles were all white wine, and yet somehow..." Steven was still replaying the evening in his mind. He ran one hand through the short thick richness of his hair. "We served red wine with the meal," he recalled with wonder. "Didn't we? Where did it all come from? They couldn't have delivered again, not in minutes."

Madeline chuckled.

Curiosity swept into his eyes and he stared at her. She broke into faltering convulsions of laughter. Her tired body ached, and the laughter hurt like dull knives stabbing into her ribs. Even she knew it wouldn't do to serve white wine with *boeuf en croûte*. It was ideal for the scallop appetizer but they had used another white wine for that and that was before the error had been discovered. There was no time. The entrée was about to be served; no one knew what to do; Steven was dragged off to perform the final plate preparations; Jessica and Lois, the inn's housekeeper, were clearing off dishes; and Diane—a local cottager pressed into service to help out—was starting to deliver the next course. Madeline was left with the thirty-six bottles of white wine, which were supposed to be red. From somewhere in the flurry of the moment, she just decided the easiest thing to do was to turn the white wine into red. Simple: a schoolchild could do it, *especially* a schoolchild.

"You didn't," Steven said with a gasp.

Madeline nodded. "It was easy, right there on the spice rack after fennel and fenugreek." Was he angry? "We could have had blue wine if you'd wanted."

"That's why it was served in carafes, instead of the bottles. You just added food coloring to the white wine?"

He started to laugh so violently he could barely sputter out, "My mother would be horrified. I'll have to tell her."

"Why?"

"Because it's funny!"

Desperate not to laugh, Madeline fought back the urge. She was tired and her sides already ached, but the inclination infected her—the thought of the elegant diners sipping bogus wine . . . She succumbed to paroxysms of childish giggling. "And the smoked scallops? How were they?"

"Good, seemed a little different than normal, but . . . Okay, what did you do to them?"

Smoking scallops was relatively easy. Madeline had followed the printed page of instructions. The scallops were already shucked, delivered fresh that afternoon by a local fisherman. In the basement storeroom, there were special tin boxes the size of small suitcases. The scallops were spread on a rack over some shavings of dry hickory. The tin boxes were sealed up and placed on hot barbecue grates for ten minutes, then taken off. The garnish called for eleven different ingredients and the greengrocer had delivered fresh ginger, sweet onions, and celery, but the mangoes were green and as hard as rocks. Madeline tried to ask Steven. He was there, but busy with endless tasks. Mangoes were a main ingredient, so she couldn't leave them out. Scouring the pantry, she discovered canned peaches—close enough.

Catching his breath, he stuttered, "Oh, I . . . I can't imagine what would have happened if you hadn't come along. How can I ever thank you?"

Madeline thought, suddenly letting her smile slip away, *Charm my mother the way you charm me. Make her smile,* but that was just a silly thought fostered by fatigue. "It was great fun," she said finally. "Quite an experience. I'm amazed you remained so calm throughout the chaos."

"Did I appear calm?"

"Yes."

"Well, I tried to at least seem relaxed; everyone was working so hard, and didn't want to ignite panic amongst the troops. It was a struggle, but I kept reminding myself there are more important things going on in the world than a dish breaking." Then he added, "Or even a *stack* of dishes."

"Poor Jessica, I thought we'd have to sweep her up off the floor too," Madeline interjected. She'd been impressed with the sensitive way Steven had handled it, with his easy smile and calm words—telling Jessica not to worry about it, and joking that she'd saved them a lot of work because there would be a lot fewer dishes to wash.

"Or doctored wine," he carried on, "or a barefoot ring bearer, or any of our other little catastrophes. I knew all along we could somehow manage to feed the hordes and they'd dance and party and have fun, and in the end the only truly important thing was Liz and Terry starting their life together with a happy, memorable wedding day."

The only important thing . . . Madeline repeated to herself. "Important," she muttered with a sinking heart. He was right: only a few things were truly important, like her mother. That was important to her. The woman was hard and cruel, sour and evil. Surely her mother couldn't be like that, surely there must be some deep kernel of love hidden somewhere . . . somewhere. She thought of the note in her pocket, a note that could only have come from Anne Shannon. Somehow her mother had discovered she was helping out at the inn. Anne had had some time to recover from the shock of the morning and still she only wanted Madeline to leave. Why? It didn't make sense. How had she hurt her mother? Why did her mother hate her?

Madeline felt weak. She pushed all thoughts of Anne Shannon away. "Important," she began carefully, "like your father."

"Yeah," Steven agreed in a voice now suddenly wistful. "Something like that certainly puts a lot of things in perspective. A few broken dishes sure don't seem very important."

Madeline continued, "You haven't heard anything yet?" She'd seen him with the phone caught in the crook of his neck several times. Each time she tried to watch his face for clues.

"He's going to be okay. I know it. But the next few days are critical."

Yes, Madeline thought, the next few days were critical for her too.

Outside the moon was up and moving slowly along the limestone path, through the gardens. The big white peonies glowed. Living in an apartment on a busy street in San Jose, Madeline had never heard quiet like this—no cars, no faraway sirens.

"You know, you haven't told me what originally brought you here."

"I wanted to meet Anne Shannon."

"Anne? Why?"

"I wanted to ask her about a book she wrote."

"Ah yes, the famous book. I bet she chased you away with her broom." He laughed.

"Sort of." Madeline's answer was curt. She wasn't sure she was ready to speak of this, but she felt compelled to ask, "Does she chase everyone away?"

"Pretty much." Steven's grin faded quickly. Shoulders curling, he offered a tired shrug. "My mother says she's just a bit eccentric. I don't know about that."

He left the thought to float in the air for a while, then when Madeline made no response he succumbed to a yawn and stretched, leaning back and closing his eyes. "I just might sleep right—" Steven abruptly stopped and turned to her. "You're not local, are you? I'm sorry, I've been so busy, I never realized..." He pushed away the table and staggered to his feet. "We have to find you a place to sleep."

"That's okay," Madeline countered as she rose.

He spied her knapsack. "You're not leaving?"

Madeline nodded. She was too worn out to develop a plan, but leaving seemed like the only thing to do.

The wedding reception was over, she was no longer needed, and Anne Shannon wanted her gone.

"No. You can't," he protested, tucking away his chair. "My mother would box my ears—after all the help you've been! What sort of innkeeper would I be, pushing you out into the night? Besides, I have a bike tour in tomorrow and a group of whale-watchers, or is it bird-watchers, or is it that crazy kayaking group? Anyway it's somebody, and quite frankly while Jessica is very nice and tries her best, she's not much use in a crunch, Lois is busy with cleaning the rooms and hates doing anything else, anything to do with people, and then there's Diane, she was terrific but she's a friend who Mom pressed into service to help us out, and..."

"I've got to go."

"You can't possibly. Where can you go?" He paused and caught his breath and spied something in her eyes, then added meaningfully, and mischievously, "You haven't really met Anne, have you? I know her quite well. I can arrange an... what shall we call it, an encounter with her, if you'd like. She'd do that for me."

"Really?" Madeline asked, unsure if that was a good idea or not. She had edged back into the lobby. "Why?"

"I have"—he tried unsuccessfully to make his voice sound deep and ominous—"special powers."

Steven turned off a series of lights. "But really, why are you so interested in her?"

Madeline was glad she was hidden by the shadows. "The book. It just struck a chord with me and I wanted to ask her a few things." Like what happened to her daughter, the daughter in the book.

"Well, I won't let you just wander off into the night. I'm sorry I can't offer you much of a bunk, but . . ."

A bunk, any bunk, or bed, or expanse of floor suddenly sounded like the epitome of decadent luxury. She had enjoyed sitting and the thought of lying down and stretching out completely horizontal was delicious. "Is there a pillow?" Madeline asked. Already she could imagine the joy of her head sinking into a big soft pillow.

"Of course."

"Oh," she moaned, "a pillow. It sounds like heaven." At that moment pillows would get her vote as the greatest invention in the history of mankind.

"And tomorrow, you can have as many pillows as you like. I'll do anything to keep you here all summer. Anything."

Madeline laughed. "I couldn't possibly."

"I'll beg. I know I've been a slave driver today, but it was a special situation. Why, tomorrow I will even give you some time off. Well, maybe not tomorrow; tomorrow is going to be another busy day, but soon." He was exhausted and rambling on, trying to make a convincing case. "There is a lot to see here, you know, whales out in the bay, and ... Have you seen the whales?"

Madeline shook her head.

He caught her response, then continued moving into the kitchen, clicking off lights as he went. "Well, you can't leave without seeing the whales, and I'll take you out sailing. And there are the reversing falls, of course, and the magnetic hill and—" At the top of the stairs he took her hand in his, then led her down into the basement.

"Do you do this for all your employees?"

"Like I said, Jessica is very nice, but ... well, I don't think we'd have much in common."

She was too tired to censor her thoughts and the words just slipped out. "But we do, you and I?"

"I think so. I hope so."

"Oh," she responded in embarrassment and surprise.

They were in the dark, winding down big rough limestone steps. Ahead a dim light glowed. "Where are you from?" he asked.

"California, San Jose."

"Really? And you've come all this way just to meet Auntie Anne?"

"Well ..."

"You must have really liked that book."

Madeline didn't answer.

He lead her to a far corner of the basement where

there was a roll-away cot neatly made up with flannel sheets, wool blanket, and a big soft feather pillow.

"Here you go. There's a little washroom in the corner over there. It should have everything you need." He smiled shyly. Evidently he had forgotten he held her hand, for as he leaned away the arms stretched taut and like an elastic band yanked him back. He wobbled, and she wobbled, both plainly tired. "Thank you," Steven said gently, then he gave her that soft, thoughtful smile again. It made her smile too.

She felt the electric touch of his hand, and it radiated sparks that multiplied exponentially and scampered along and down the ribbons of her trembling nerves and tired muscles. Madeline all but collapsed into his arms. She craved the warmth and soothing comfort she knew lay in his embrace, but she wouldn't allow that to happen and instead slipped away to sit on the edge of her cot.

"Good night," he murmured. After a slight hesitation he was gone and all of a sudden she was alone.

Without much preparation she scuttled in between the cozy sheets and her heavy eyelids sagged and closed. Plunging into the depths of sleep, she contemplated the luck of finding an empty bed in the tightly packed little inn. *This was his bed,* she realized with a start. *Probably the last bed anywhere.* She was too tired to think or move anymore. The impulse to rise, to find him and protest, surfaced in her mind, but it never had a chance. She was too tired, and every thought sank away as Madeline fell asleep.

Chapter Five

Two more steps and she could see over the ledge, and there he was, hunched forward, reading instructions from a sheet of paper as he used a big wooden spoon to beat batter in a stainless-steel bowl. She caught herself smiling. Rumpled, drowsy, a trifle disheveled, yet as he looked up and smiled shyly, she felt he was more delightful than possible. She loved his sparkling eyes, his soft cheek dusted with whole-wheat flour. She liked his full and gentle mouth too, the easy fluid way he moved, and his cap of thick, toussled brown hair, replete, this morning, with a wayward tuft standing out behind one ear. She liked him. He brought happiness into her heart. It was beyond simple; she liked everything about him. And his smile made her morning anguish melt away and, despite her

Death and Deception 43

efforts to maintain a tight reign, her heart leaped up and sang.

The spoon slowed and stopped. He looked at her and said softly, "Yesterday wasn't a dream—you really do exist. My beautiful angel of mercy returns."

"Don't mock me," Madeline countered. She didn't feel that looking rumpled, as she knew she did, would embellish her appearance the way it did his. "I'm a mess is what I am."

Steven interrupted, protesting, "Angels can only wish they looked half as sweet as you." Suddenly the effervescence waned and he seemed to sink back with creeping shyness. Madeline wondered if he might be blushing. Was it possible she could make such a man blush? He looked away, back to his batter, content for the moment to watch it swirl.

"I took your bed, didn't I?"

"No," he protested feebly. "No."

"I did."

"Well..." His shoulders rose up, his head canted to one side. "That's okay."

Here comes that gentle smile, Madeline calculated. *The one that starts in his eyes and there, there it is.* She knew him. It had only been one day, and yet it felt like she'd known him all her life. They both instantly anticipated each other's needs and strategies. They could communicate with just a word, a nod, or a glance. She was drawn to him, she didn't know why, and she didn't dare think it was possible he might be equally drawn to her, but Madeline couldn't stop it. Fearing she was becoming mesmerized, she had to look away.

He glanced down at his batter and gave it another twirl.

Timers were merrily ticking away. Things were sizzling in pans all around her. Madeline began to flip peameal bacon, then she rolled over sausages. "Any word about your father?"

He slowed and studied the batter. "Dad had a quiet night. So far, so good." It was only a ghost of a smile now. Picking up the bowl, he tipped it and poured some onto the hot griddle. "Hungry?"

"Mmm, starving."

"I think everyone is sleeping in this morning."

"That's good."

"They're all leaving today and I have to get the place ready for the . . ." He looked across the kitchen and squinted at the calendar. "The Rolling Thunder bike tour company. They'll probably straggle in around three, tired and sweaty, but mostly hungry and usually very thirsty." Four large pancakes were spluttering on the griddle. "Hors d'oeuvres at fourish. How are you at tending bar?"

"Never done it before, so about as good as I am at cooking or waiting tables."

"Great." He drew the word out long and deep and she wondered if he was being sarcastic, but decided he was just gently teasing. "I knew I could count on you."

The pancakes were four perfect circles, so he stopped pouring and placed the bowl up on the center shelf. "Can you make a strawberry daiquiri? We have fresh strawberries."

"No, but I had one once."

"Great," he said again, drawing the word out playfully. Then he added a short laugh.

"If it's in that bartender's book, I guess I can." With Steven around it was easy to feel like you could do anything.

"And we have Venture Tours, a bus group. They do some whale watching in the morning, stop in here for brunch around eleven-fifteen, then they're out and on their way to Nova Scotia by noon."

"I'm amazed you can juggle all this."

"Well, occasionally a few items crash to the floor, but so far no fatalities." On top of the hectic learning of all the sundry aspects of running a small country inn, he had the added stress of worrying about his father.

Madeline's thoughts shifted to the source of *her* worries, *her* stress: Anne Shannon. Amazingly, she rekindled a little warmth. Somewhere during her sound sleep a new idea had germinated, the idea that maybe a youthful mistake could lead to the abandonment of an infant daughter and that coupled with the passage of a long, lonely time could sour a naturally sweet mother—the wonderful mother of the book. Undoubtedly there was much more to the story than the little bit she had so far discovered. Despair might drive a mother to forsake a child; there could be clear and logical reasons to do it. Intellectually, Madeline understood that, but understanding was not accepting, and it was hard to just gleefully get on with life. Led to believe her mother had drowned, over the years Madeline allowed herself less and less time to pine about the loss. She was alone; there was no family to help her. Anything she got out of life she knew she'd have to work for. Focusing first on her schooling, then her career, she lost herself in work, refusing to waste time feeling sorry for herself, never looking aside and wondering. But discovering the book changed all that.

Now she was faced with the overwhelming evidence that her mother was alive and had created an elaborate ruse to abandon her. And what was worse, despite turning her life around and becoming a successful author, Anne Shannon had never come back, never tried to make any contact at all. Maybe it was shame. Maybe she thought it best not to interfere. But what possible reason could a woman have for rejecting her daughter now? Madeline wanted nothing from her mother, certainly nothing more than she herself had to offer in exchange.

The past was gone. Madeline didn't concern herself with it; she wasn't going to judge or blame. There could be good reasons for what had happened. But somehow she had to know the whole story, otherwise she knew it would become a shadow lurking over her for the rest of her life. It would sour her. It might turn her into a cold and bitter witch... like her mother? The specter, she realized, was already there, locked in place. There was only one way to vanquish it. She wouldn't allow herself to be chased away; she had to dig out all the answers.

Steven flipped the pancakes. Madeline began to stir home fries. A big fruit salad was on the counter, and four trays of warm muffins, which Steven began to turn out and arrange in baskets. One of the infernal timers began to buzz. It was close to Madeline, so she plucked it up, turned it off, and looked at the sheet of paper beneath.

"Enough food here for an army," she mentioned as she read.

"We've only begun. There is a big brunch every Sunday; I forgot to mention that. Most of the people from the wedding reception will be back, and probably a little hung over from too much white wine." He caught her eyes, then added, "Plus the bus tour, most of the cottagers, and a few of the locals come after church. It's sort of the neighborhood's traditional Sunday morning hangout. Pretty popular."

Madeline listened while she snooped into the ovens. A huge ham was roasting in one, two beef roasts were in another, pies in the two above.

"You made the pies?" She dropped open the door. Using oven mitts, she slid them out, one at a time.

"No, thank goodness, for the brunch a local woman does. We just have to bake them."

As the last pie dropped onto the counter, Steven began to refill the oven with more. He brushed across her back. Like a cat, she felt herself respond involuntary. Silly—the contact had been so faint, and unintentional; nonetheless it caused a warm shiver and a sudden craving. She found she had stopped working; she'd turned to him and was staring.

Steven fell into her eyes. She was willing him closer. Slowly he came ahead. He placed his hand lightly upon her shoulder. A tickle wakened and warmed. She was no longer drowsy. The fuzzy cobwebs vanished. Her tired limbs were humming. Her skin was alive. Her heart began to thud.

She had sensed from the moment she saw him that he was someone special; she was going to know him forever. At first she railed against the feeling. So little had been said or done, and yet in an instant the thought would leap from impossible to inevitable. With every moment they'd been together the thought strengthened. Despite being forcefully banished from her mind time and time again, it nevertheless stayed and grew and flourished—her life had fundamentally changed. She was thrilled and terrified. Socially, she felt inept. Too much time had been spent in the company of textbooks and computers and not enough socializing, practically never with men.

Satisfied with her response to his real, vivid, yet unspoken question, his head tipped to one side as he slipped closer, slowly, ever so slowly, giving Madeline every opportunity to withdraw. But why would she? How could she resist this delicious man, warm, sensitive, gorgeous, and kind?

She had never been impulsive; her life felt precarious enough. Never did she feel she could take risks or liberties, not until she chanced upon the book. Discovering that book had turned everything inside down and upside out.

Madeline allowed her eyes to close. His lips trailed across the rise of her cheek. Their lips touched. The kiss, only one, only for one heart-stopping instant, was everything possible, including nice and warm and comfortable—patient, as if to say this was too precious to rush. Or perhaps he was just shy, or sensed that she was. For whatever reason, he soon eased away. Her head swimming, she too drew back, not scared, but feeling an urge to shudder. She wanted to feel his warm arms envelop her, to possess his lips once more. And perversely she wanted to run away.

They exchanged timid smiles, both aware that this was exquisite, this was bliss, but one innocent kiss and things were already beginning to teeter out of control. It wasn't the time or the place. While each knew they wanted that kiss, they didn't know what to do next.

They hardly knew each other. But it was a kiss, and now new rules were established. They were no longer just friends or kitchen comrades. She had never been party to anything like it, such instant communication, such understanding and compassion. She had never met a man like Steven, had never even dreamed someone like him might exist. A simple kiss, a smile, and they understood and respected each other.

The pancakes were burning. Steven flipped one off the griddle, then swiftly added the others. As he poked at the brown crust with the spatula, he quipped, "Great," and again he drew the word out long and slow. "Should have set the timer. I guess these must be mine."

"I'd love to help you," Madeline announced with wide eyes and a pat on her stomach.

They sat facing each other at the little table in the corner, passing back maple syrup, fresh strawberries, and orange juice. Madeline found herself staring at him too much; their eyes kept locking. She struggled to relax. She struggled to catch her breath. Close beyond the window was the herb garden; a chipmunk stood on the stone walkway. Madeline watched, happy for the distraction. Confused, the chipmunk skittered one way, then the other. Looking up at her, he stared back, frozen, then vanished.

They ate, first in silence, then, after a timer sent him on a brief foray back to the ovens, Steven said, "This morning I spoke to my mother about all this."

"About all what?"

"You. Anne. The book."

"Oh." Madeline felt herself shrinking. She wasn't ready to deal with Anne, the book.

"Mom thanks you for the help—the peaches and the food coloring, and whatnot, especially the quick thinking. She was horrified, then, laughed till it hurt. She wished she could have been here to see it. She's really looking forward to meeting you."

"I . . ." Madeline shrugged.

"She takes the inn very seriously. Not that it's a big business, or a money thing. I'm sure it doesn't make much money, but keeping the place running for people to enjoy is sort of a responsibility for her."

"It's very special."

"Some people claim the Harbourview was the first resort established anywhere in the Maritimes. You know, there's a book about it tracing the history, the various owners, and the entire cottage colony, the chapel—some famous people have been married there. Anyway, if you mess up, it's forever recorded."

"Maybe they'll add a chapter about your heroic efforts," Madeline quipped.

"I'm already in there, just as an extra, not for being in any way heroic or anything, just for helping out from time to time. Now you will be in there too."

"No," she scoffed.

"It's a sure thing." He refilled their cups with tea.

Madeline laughed a little. She brought her teacup to

her lips but before she took a drink she said, "Tell me about Anne." She took a sip. "How well do you know her?"

"Not well, but I guess better than almost anyone, except my parents, and Lois, of course." He shrugged again. Aware that she hung on his every word and hoped for more, he searched for any scrap he could add. "For as long as I can remember she has always lived in that stone cottage. And from what I've heard, mostly from my mother, Auntie Anne had a pretty wild early life—you know, in her teens and twenties. She ran away from home, disappeared for years, traveled everywhere, did everything, the seventies kind of stuff. Now I think maybe she's burned out, a bit of a recluse, though she makes herself at home around the inn and the gardens, all the locals do, but I don't think she goes much beyond this neighborhood. Even lives here in the winter, though almost everything else shuts down. My parents leave; they've got a place in Arizona." He ate the last of his pancakes. "For a long time everyone figured Anne was busily working on her next book. But there never was another book. At least not one that I heard of."

Another timer went off and Steven stood, gathering up the dirty dishes. "If there is something in particular you want to know about, I could ask my mom. Or you could try Lois, if you're feeling brave, but she can be just as cranky as Anne."

"Lois?" Madeline asked. It was the second time Steven had mentioned her in connection to Anne.

"She and Anne are longtime buddies. I don't know how far back. Quite a pair."

Madeline thought for a moment. The two women were similar. She'd worked with Lois the night before; the woman was tall and thin with straight salt-and-pepper hair cut short in a sort of Prince Valiant–style haircut, and she was just as silent and distant as Anne had been.

"I guess I'm just curious about the book and the trip, mostly. How much is true, how much she made up. That sort of thing. Did she ever get married, have children? There was a little girl in the book."

"I doubt it. Something like that I would have heard about." He shrugged. "Now, don't look so worried, I'll arrange for you to meet her. I'm sure she'll do it for me. After all, what can the harm be? You seem harmless enough." As he turned away she caught the late-blooming smile again.

What harm, indeed? Madeline wondered. She called after him. "When?"

Steven thought for a moment and said flatly, "Last day of the summer season, Labor Day weekend."

"What?" Madeline gasped.

"Well, it was worth a try." He laughed. "Okay, how about as soon as possible, but promise me you won't run off right after."

Madeline knew better than to promise. She kept

changing her plans, but at that moment she was pretty sure she wouldn't be leaving any time soon.

Steven returned and sat. "Tomorrow is Monday; things will quiet down a bit. There's a bridge club here in the afternoon, but they're regulars; they pretty well serve themselves. So, tomorrow sometime, maybe around ten. How's that?" Steven noted her response; he watched her slow, serious, almost frightened nod. "Now then." He took a sip of his tea. "I need to know all about you."

Her eyes shot away, evading his. "There isn't much to tell," Madeline began. Telling people about her life was something she avoided. She disliked incurring the heavy weight of their pity. You couldn't tell someone you were left as an orphan at the age of five, and adopted, and that it didn't work out, without them asking why and wanting details, and without everyone feeling uncomfortable and sympathetic. She didn't want to relive the past. And she certainly didn't want, or need, or deserve, anyone's pity. Madeline considered herself luckier than most. She had intelligence and good health. She knew she was reasonably attractive. And while she occasionally thought it would be nice to be a little taller, she realized that that was a very petty desire. She just grew up without a real family around; that's all there was to it. Many people had far more serious problems.

"Come on. I know you live in California and, let's

see, you're an avid reader—you must be. Is this the first time you've flown off to meet an author?"

"Yes."

"This book was that special to you?"

"It just struck a chord."

Steven looked at her. She could feel his skepticism.

"I always wanted to visit the East Coast anyway, antiques and *Anne of Green Gables* and all that." The truth was she had never even heard of New Brunswick until she started digging around researching the author Anne Shannon. And while she vaguely knew the story *Anne of Green Gables,* she didn't know the details until she picked up a Prince Edward Island tourism brochure while waiting at the Saint John bus station.

"Do you have a job?"

"Yes." This was safe ground; no need for troublesome little white lies. "I work for Imagine X. We produce computer software, animation, mostly."

"Really? That sounds like fun."

"Yes." She smiled self-consciously. "It is. I write code mostly, you know, programming. We've just finished a CD-ROM game called 'True to Life.' It gets released this summer."

"Great." He waited. "And?"

"And what?" Madeline asked. "That's about it."

His brow furrowed. "Family?"

"No," was her curt reply. Her discomfort rising, she worked to avoid his gaze. Steven quite likely had never met anyone without any family relations. For her, while growing up, it had been the norm. Then she added, with a valiant but faltering smile, "None to speak of."

"None?" His voice quavered with surprise. She could see him puzzling over what she had said. None to speak of? What did that mean? She wished she hadn't added that.

Another timer went off. Steven hesitated before reluctantly returning to the bank of ovens. Madeline took the opportunity to gather up the last of the dishes and then she went to the big steel sinks. Last night's roasting pans, the ones she had left to soak, were gone, scrubbed clean and shiny, now hanging on their hooks.

"Don't worry about the dishes," Steven announced, just as Jessica arrived. She came through the swinging doors and slipped out of her jacket. Steven called out, "Good morning," as he handed Madeline two big galvanized buckets and a pair of garden shears. "Here you go." He nodded to a row of vases. "For the brunch table. So cut anything you want, but only from out back." He steered her out the back door, then he turned to Jessica and they began to talk.

The formal gardens were in front and to one side of the inn. Out beyond the small herb garden were rows of flowers, vegetables, and even some fruit trees, a strawberry patch, and a long row of raspberry canes.

Madeline wandered. Stopping, she bent down to snip a few white carnations. There was something he had said about Anne Shannon that, at the time, seemed surprising and potentially important. But as she thought it over—recluse, enigma, well traveled, but travels no more, cranky, mysterious—these were all things she already knew.

One bucket was quickly full. It was pleasant cutting flowers; the colors were cheerful, the air a blend of perfume and rich black dirt, the work gentle and relaxing.

Madeline felt a swell of guilt rising within her. Steven had quickly become her safe harbor in the dizzying storm, so it was unfair to hold back secrets. Besides, he was too intuitive not to suspect there was a lot more than what she had told him. She should tell him everything, she knew that, but she was scared. She thought of kissing him again, then envisioned being snug in his arms. "I was just relaxing, and reading Anne's book; it was good, but my mind kept wandering, you know how it is sometimes when a book makes you think of other things, things in your own life, and this one did. I thought I might be the daughter—you know, in the book. It was fun at first, then scary, then I thought I must be going crazy." *No, I would never say that to Steven, not "going crazy."*

She shuddered. Even to her it did seem sort of crazy.

Chapter Six

The air was still. Thick trees filtered the glowing moonlight and they walked slowly through the gentle shadows, side by side, hand in hand. Steven had Madeline's knapsack slung over his shoulder as he led her along the gravel lane toward the bay.

It had been another good and hectic day. Judging by the vast stacks of dirty dishes, brunch had been a great success. Then the bike tour arrived, mostly happy young seniors. They ate well, drank only modestly, laughed and joked, and turned in for the night early. The next day they had a fairly long cycle ahead of them along the coast road to Back Bay, where they were taking the ferry to Grand Manan Island.

"Where are we going?" Madeline asked again. She'd assumed he'd find her a corner of the inn to sleep in, perhaps the same cot in the basement; that would be fine.

"Be patient, just a little surprise, trust me."

Beyond the hedges and bushes there were the summer cottages. Again she wondered if they could be headed to Anne Shannon's. He seemed to know her well—how well? Well enough to impose like that? But no, Madeline realized with relief, even in the darkness she was reasonably certain the Shannon cottage was up the other way.

They were almost at the beach; she could see silver light shimmering on the black water beyond. Steven pushed open a rough wooden gate. Half hidden behind a screen of bushes thick with tiny white blossoms there was a cabin with, she discerned as they drew closer, big windows and wood siding that looked old and weather worn. It was sun-bleached white and the grain stood up proudly like corduroy.

"Whose—?"

Steven had unlocked the back door, and gave it a sharp jolt to force it open, then he reached in and switched on the light. "Bit rustic—no, not rustic, casual. Nice, isn't it?"

It was very small and already Steven had placed her knapsack on the kitchen table and passed into the living room area. "Lois gave it a quick cleanup this morning, so it just needs a bit of airing out." He slid open a glass door that led to a small deck that overlooked the water. Fresh sea air flooded in.

Madeline looked out the front window at the bay. "Whose is it?"

"The Barbours', Pete and Maggie. They're traveling in Europe this summer." He waited while she looked around. "Many of the cottagers ask us to oversee rental of their places while they're not using them. So, here you are. It's yours for as long as I can keep you."

"It's . . ." She swung slowly around, inspecting the plank flooring, throw rugs, and rough wood beams. There was a wicker basket on the counter with tea and cookies and fruit. It was mostly one long room, sort of a living room/dining room/kitchen, with two doors off to the side, one leading to a small bedroom at the water's edge and the other to a large and surprisingly sumptuous washroom with separate stall shower and whirlpool tub. "Wow. It's perfect, but are you sure it's okay?"

"Of course, all taken care of." There was no reason to question him further. He knew everyone. He even knew her mother, knew her much better than she herself did.

"Big day tomorrow." Madeline frowned. She wasn't hopeful.

"Anne is expecting you at ten."

A shiver had worked its way up into her shoulders. She was scared. More than ever, she thought she might want his arms snug and warm around her. Since the kiss that morning they hadn't so much as accidentally brushed each other.

He was near. She could feel his aura warm and close behind her. There was much more tension than there had been that morning. This time it would be awkward to break away, and impossible not to kiss him. She might go crazy if she did not touch him soon. She wished she weren't so nervous; she wished she could catch her breath, control her diverse thoughts.

Turning, he was there, expectant, smiling softly, breathing her name. In his eyes a question was being asked. Madeline answered by rising up on her toes to meet him, by allowing her lips to be captured by his.

But Madeline faltered. Even as she was exhilarating in the moment, she was searching through all the possible reasons why she shouldn't be doing this. From somewhere a niggling fear had awakened, stirred, and reared up. Something so wonderful must have a cost, that was her inclination, but ... what could the harm be? Steven was wonderful; he was handsome, warm, and sensitive. He wasn't the type to hurt anyone, at least not intentionally. What could the harm be? He had arranged tomorrow's meeting; he cared about her. Her mind was in turmoil. She thought of all these things, she thought of everything all at once, until her her mind was imploding and she thought of nothing. She gave in to the moment. She let herself go free. Their lips parted. She gave up all control; she was content to be whisked away on the surging current.

He was wonderful. He was everything she could possibly want. He'd even taken charge of her dealings with Anne Shannon; it was like him, so nice, so considerate, but how had he managed that? A funny little stream of anxiety floated into her mind. Why would Anne do it for him? How did he know her so well?

Sinking back from her tiptoe position, Madeline slipped from his grasp. Fear gripped her heart. Suddenly, she twisted away and stiffened. Her arms crowded up between them. "I'm sorry, I can't..."

He responded softly, honestly, without rancor. "You can't kiss a man who has fallen in love with you?" Anguish replaced the pleasure in his eyes, but there was no trace of anger.

"I'm sorry," Madeline stammered.

There was a long and awkward pause. "No, it's my fault," Steven countered. "I misunderstood. I thought, I thought..." He was confused. She could see his every thought pass through his eyes—he did love her.

How to explain? She had to explain.

"Madeline, I would never—"

Auntie Anne, he had said. Auntie Anne. She remembered it clearly now, and while at first she hadn't fathomed the consequences, now she did. Steven would be family, her cousin. He was no longer smiling, just dazed and disappointed, and Madeline felt the same. She desperately wanted to confide in him, but she had no experience with confiding. She didn't know how. She was afraid she'd start to cry, and she didn't know how to cry with people around. She didn't know if she could stop. Crying, unable to stop—that terrified her. She'd feel silly and weak and helpless.

It was agony to fall in love so quickly, so mutually, so powerfully, so totally, for the first time, only to realize that romantic love was out of the question.

"Maybe you're right," Steven announced, after he'd waited a long time. She could tell he was unconvinced. He was trying hard to understand. Reaching out, he took her forearms in his hands and gave a tender squeeze. "I guess I'd better go." And he backed away, slipping out the door and into the shadows. Abruptly, he was gone.

Madeline stood and stared into the night. Then she shut the door and paced nervously, only to find herself stopped and standing on the front deck gazing out at the water, trying to regain her equilibrium. She felt crushed. The world continued to play tricks on her. A mother who didn't want her; at last a love—he'd said that he'd fallen in love with her, hadn't he? But he would be her first cousin. It wasn't fair.

She could gather up her knapsack and leave now, return to the safe and lonely cocoon she had established in California. She could probably catch a late bus and be on a flight before anyone, before Steven, discovered her gone in the morning. She could do that and spend the rest of her life wondering. She wasn't a quitter; the inclination to give up flashed into her mind and she thought a moment, then quashed it. Always in the past she would grit her teeth and fight on.

This time the situation was truly hopeless. How could she fight? Where was she supposed to direct her energies? What could hard work do for her? It was frustrating, beyond frustrating—it was maddening.

But her mother . . . She had to know the truth, whatever the cost. And if not now, when? If she ran, she'd never risk returning again. This was it. What more could she possibly lose? She would try once more, but only once. If there was no progress she'd close the book on this misadventure and begin the long trek home, and attempt to put everything behind her. She tried to convince herself she didn't need family, she didn't need Steven.

Madeline flung herself on the bed. For one wild and absurd instant, the possibility of keeping her relationship with Anne Shannon a secret flashed in her mind. That was the only bar to the comforting warmth of Steven's embrace. She should just keep it secret.

Cousins? Cousins! She pounded the pillow. Was that why she felt so instantly connected with Steven? She had found family; should she be happy? But she couldn't find any joy at all. In fact, once again her loneliness felt complete.

Alone and too tired to resist, she bit the inside of her cheek. She had much to cry about. All of her life she had striven to be a strong, independent woman, and against the odds she had succeeded. Now she was reduced to heartrending, babbling confusion. If having family caused this ripping apart of her soul then maybe she was better off alone. Alone, she had never suffered such terrible pain.

Chapter Seven

Half an hour later exhaustion won out over anxiety, but not before a bout of supine calisthenics had rendered the once neat and cozy bed a knotted mass of arms and legs and rolled-up bedding. The night blackened. A haze formed around the moon. The air grew cool and wet with dew. Madeline kicked. One leg had strayed from the duvet's warmth; cool toes tickled Madeline half-awake. She flailed about, trying to bring her wandering appendages back into the nest.

She shuddered and stirred. There was something else, a strange feeling. Was she alone? Overwhelmed by a feeling of urgency, she struggled to waken. Something felt odd.

From beyond the window screen came the low murmur of the tide rubbing along the shore; otherwise all seemed quiet. Neither the strange room nor the different bed disturbed her—she found everything remarkably comfortable and the cool moist air delicious. Still, she was reluctant to just roll over and fall asleep again. Something had disturbed her, she didn't know what. It wasn't just cold toes. Still groggy, Madeline squirmed to lift her head and pry open her eyes. Perhaps Steven had returned to look in. Maybe he had dropped by after things finished up at the inn to see if she was still awake. Maybe he had decided it was time for an explanation.

She strained to listen, holding her breath, then whispered his name.

Nothing was visible in the near-perfect blackness, but near at hand there was something, a living presence, breathing. She could feel it in the air, taste it.

"Steven," she said, even though she knew it couldn't possibly be him. There was no answer. Finally, she chanced a breath.

Raunchy, like an animal... For all the world it felt like a hot wet breath was gushing upon her face, like steam, a foul and fetid mist. Madeline tensed. She struggled with logical explanations. She reached for the table lamp. A frenetic scratching and scuffling broke the silence. She recoiled. Then a growl erupted, almost a snarl. Scrunching her body up small, she rolled away into the corner. She screamed.

There was a sharp quick yelp, immediately followed by nails skittering on the wood floor.

Madeline screamed again, louder this time. She flailed her legs. She yanked the covers up to protect her face then pulled her feet in under herself and stiffened, expecting an onslaught of teeth and razor-sharp claws.

Instead the screen door banged. Still Madeline waited. She was gasping for breath and struggling with her nerves. Cautiously lowering her blankets, she searched the darkness. She could see nothing. Nonetheless, she screamed once more, a scream to release the residual terror that kept building up within her.

It was deathly quiet again, dreamlike, but she was sure it was real, it had happened—a dog, some big dog had been there in her room, in the blackness, right before her eyes, close to her face, while she slept. She gasped again.

Feeling the need for action, she rocked forward onto her feet. Slapping the wall in search of the light switch, she found it. She was alone. Flush against the wall, she waited, listening; the rest of the cottage seemed empty. She slipped into the living room and found a lamp and turned it on. She was indeed alone. The back door was closed. The back door was locked. She was certain she had locked it after Steven. The dog hadn't wandered in, he hadn't opened the door, and he hadn't locked the door behind himself. Either she had dreamed the dog—she *hadn't* dreamed it, she knew she hadn't dreamed it—or the dog had a partner. It must, of course; there was a human partner.

Anne, who else but Anne? Who else could there be behind this and every other inexplicable disaster that befell her?

Soon Madeline had every light on in the small building. Every closet was checked, behind the furniture and under the bed and the kitchen counter. No squirrels, or mice, or lost puppies; she was alone. On the wall by the refrigerator she found a phone and picked it up, intending to call Steven. Call him and say what? Tell him a fantastic tale of a dog in the dark, a dog that woke her, a huge dog—in her mind he was huge—a huge dog she never did see that breathed on her face and made strange noises, but never attacked or barked or even touched her, a dog that just vanished through a locked door. No. Steven might question her sanity. She was questioning her own sanity. He'd certainly have questions, many questions. Besides, she was safe now. The dog was gone and she wasn't going out into the night after it.

Instead Madeline made sure again that all the doors and windows were locked. She got the largest knife she could find from the kitchen and returned to the bedroom. She pushed her bed up against the door. Then leaving the light on, she lay there propped up on the pillows and waited for morning.

Someone wanted to frighten her, that was all, she gradually concluded. They'd succeeded. They hadn't tried to do more than scare her. They could have, easily; after all, she was asleep and they were in the room with her. Obviously, they only wanted to scare her into leaving. But why was someone—Anne Shannon, who else could it be—so determined to scare her away?

She didn't try to sleep. Thoughts flitted by but they were distressing thoughts. There was a horrible throbbing in her heart, something she had never felt before, at least not in many years. Her emotions, long locked away like in some cold steel vault, were free. Steven, even more so than the book, had burst the vault open. But she couldn't deal with the torrent of feelings. It hurt. Thoughts kept flying at her, ravaging her heart. She couldn't take any more.

There was a dog, wasn't there? There was a book, and a trip, a trip that she had taken, identical to the one in the book; she had the pictures. Anne Shannon must be her mother.

And Steven was her cousin. She wasn't going crazy; it just felt like it.

By the time Madeline got up and moved the bed back from the door, the blackness of night had faded to a thick hazy gray. The sun may have risen in the east, but so far there was no sign of it in her small kitchen. She made tea.

Sitting at the table, she flipped open a brown file folder. Maybe she had missed something; that was the hope that kept sneaking into her mind. She'd go over it all again. The top page was her summary. If this was school and a test was coming up, she'd have called it her cheat sheet, a quick refresher containing just the hard facts. Madeline skimmed through her notes, hoping somehow something had changed during the night, but the facts didn't change. They were clear and pointed in one direction only. Anne Shannon was her mother and Steven Raven was her cousin.

On the top page was written:

1. Mother born Pamela Sue Paige, May 24, 1947, in Syracuse, New York. Source of information: my birth certificate, her birth certificate, police records, Internet inquiries.

Madeline took a sip of hot tea. Meeting her mother again this morning felt every bit like a college exam. She would confront the woman with the facts. This time she didn't really need a last-minute cram or her cheat sheet. In fact, rarely at college had she needed either, not from a knowledge point of view, but it focused her attention. Studying she found soothing. Work was always relaxing.

From the front zip pocket of the knapsack she took out a small plastic folder about the size of a wallet. It was a photo album. The shots were poor quality: old, faded, small black-and-white Polaroids. Most were of Madeline herself; only three showed her mother. She studied the slim young woman with very long, straight, dark hair that covered most of her face like a tattered curtain. It was impossible to say for certain that the vivacious young woman in these pictures was Anne Shannon. Too much time had passed. It was equally impossible to say that she wasn't.

For the thousandth time Madeline delved back into her memory trying to see her mother again. When you are four or five years old and you see your mother every day, you don't stare at her memorizing every feature in case she disappears for twenty years. She didn't even remember the color of her mother's eyes. She couldn't conjure up an image beyond the old snapshots. But when she had stood at the stone house waiting for Anne to answer the door, she thought there would be something, some spark of recognition, some little indescribable clue that would register, click deep in her mind, and she would know it was her mother. When she saw Anne Shannon, it didn't happen.

2. Madeline born September 1, 1970, in New York City. Mother would be twenty-three. Father listed as Paul Haines. Source of information: birth certificates, police records, Internet.

She looked at what she had written. Her father's story had been easier to discover. It was short, sad, and well documented. With the help of the Internet, she had discovered:

3. Paul Haines was born in Casenovia, New York. He had avoided the draft, dropping out of sight for a couple of years in the late sixties, only to turn himself in to authorities at Buffalo, New York, April 1970. He was immediately inducted into the Army and died in Vietnam, August 1972.

Had he come to Canada as a draft dodger and met Anne Shannon? She was speculating now, and she knew it, but beyond the scantest facts speculation was all she had. Maybe, discovering he was going to be a father, Paul Haines wanted to clear his name back in the States and went back to serve his time.

4. The trip in the book took place in the spring of 1974. Madeline was then three; her mother would be twenty-seven. Source of information: photographs, police files, the book Travels with Toots.

There were no dates in the book, but incidents, like the Arab oil embargo, and Mardi Gras in New Orleans, served to pinpoint when the trip had occurred. They corresponded exactly with the little stack of Polaroid pictures Madeline treasured. The book began in New York City in winter. The mother and daughter in the story packed a Chevy van with a plastic cooler and a propane camp stove, a slab of foam for a bed, and orange crates filled with books and food and clothes and eight-track tapes. They set off for Florida, arriving just as the effects of the OPEC oil embargo peaked.

Then after a series of adventures, mostly misadventures, they reached California in May.

5. Pamela Sue Paige disappeared in July 1975. Last seen parked near Moonstone Beach, California. Source of information: police records.

By now Madeline was almost five, and while she didn't clearly recall the events of her odyssey across America with her mother, she did have strong feelings about those horrific summer days after her mother disappeared. The van was parked on a cliff on the side of the coast highway above a secluded beach. While Madeline slept, it was presumed her mother went for an early morning swim and was swept away by the undertow. The body was never found. Most of all Madeline remembered the ensuing days of emptiness, the strangers staring at her and talking to her and murmuring among themselves, pretending that everything was going to be all right, nobody knowing what to do. It was an emptiness that faded but never really went away.

Copies of the police files were easy to obtain. She found the men and women there helpful and sympathetic; it was one of the rare times she openly discussed her past. The file was closed as an accidental death, financial problems were itemized, and suicide was hinted at.

6. The police report listed everything found in the van from a portable television and a transistor radio, right down to articles of clothing, and two empty wine bottles with candles stuck in the necks.

There was no mention of a typewriter, and no stack of printed pages, no manuscript awaiting discovery, just a small notebook of poetry, and over the years that was lost.

7. The book Travels with Toots *was published in 1979, written by a Canadian, Anne Shannon. It was a precise recount of the trip I took with my mother.*

That was four years after her mother had disappeared, four years after she'd been presumed drowned.

8. Conclusions: To work in the United States my mother, Anne Shannon, obtained false identification as Pamela Sue Paige. She staged her own disappearance and apparent death. She resurfaced thousands of miles away as Anne Shannon, and wrote the book Travels with Toots.

These were the bold facts, and the scenario she would confront Anne Shannon with, but there was a lot more. Madeline stood up and went to the kitchen.

She leaned on the counter and gazed out the window at the murky gray dawn.

When Madeline had chanced upon the book, and started to wonder about it, the most logical conclusion was that someone had discovered something her mother had written, either notes or a complete manuscript, and decided to pass it off as their own. But there was no manuscript. If someone had stolen something from the van, wouldn't they have taken the radio, the tapes, the little bit of money, the portable television? A stack of papers would just look like so much trash.

Travels with Toots was a paperback Madeline had innocently purchased at a neighbor's yard sale. She had only picked it up because she felt awkward browsing and not buying anything. Something about the title attracted her, and then the jacket copy explained the book was about a mother and a daughter and a trip across the southern states in an old Chevy van—something she knew she'd done with her mother years ago.

She began to read and each page began to play a little more with her mind. First it was just pangs and twinges of remembrance—the coincidences were fun and greatly exciting. But soon there were too many similarities; it became unsettling and eerie. She kept flipping to the back page and the author's bio—it was no one she knew, and the title page indicated the book was published in 1979; it was impossible. Her carefully controlled and insular life was sent careening in all directions. She had no idea what was going on.

Prior to reading the book, she didn't even know she was lonely, or wanted a family. A mother? She hadn't allowed herself to miss her until she realized the woman was alive and well. She had to be. No one else could have written this book—how could they?

Because it was hard to categorize the book, it took a couple of years to become popular. A strange hybrid, reviewers called it: fact, fiction, whimsy, raw Americana, "Zen and the art of wandering," "Catcher in the Chevy." It was definitely philosophy, and had a great deal to say about America, Americans, love, and life. It was fresh; it was insightful; it was delightfully naive. On each page, the southern locale, the endless parade of garage mechanics, the wide interstate highways and thin country back roads, strip malls and pizza parlors, deserts, mountains, and mosquitoes all became real. Most of all, it was about Toots and her mother, and love.

Like the eight-track tapes, portions of the book were dated by the time Madeline read it, but from the moment she finished the first chapter she knew her world was shifting underfoot. It was like meeting long-lost ghosts. Her once murky past was alive and she was seeing the scenes and incidents with crisp clarity.

How much did Madeline remember of her trip with her mother? Little or none, she had to admit. In fact it surprised her that she had no recollection of a day spent at Disney World. But the book detailed it—a squishy hug from Minnie, laughter on the Teacups, unexpected terror on Mr. Toad's Wild Ride.

Madeline flipped through the worn snapshots. She had no pictures of Disney World, but the book explained the camera wasn't purchased until a few days later at a K Mart near Clearwater Beach, and there was a picture of Madeline on the sand and another of the two of them together. The best picture of her mother was a group photo under a huge spreading tree at the Alamo. It surprised her that there were no pictures at all in the book; travel adventure books usually had pictures. At first she thought it might be because she had the paperback edition. But at a library she found the original hardcover. There were no pictures there either. There wasn't even a photo of the author, just a short biography: *Anne Shannon has settled down in Saint Andrew's-by-the-Sea, New Brunswick, Canada, to work on her second book.*

Perhaps the most telling snapshot was of the van jacked up high and the entire rear axle missing, with Madeline standing in front, eyes closed, smirking happily, clowning for the camera. But if you looked beyond the giggling little girl you could see black soot up the white side of the van. In the background there were pine trees and in the corner of the photo a tall sign proclaiming SPUR. Madeline had no idea what the picture was about until she read the book.

They were traveling through the emptiest part of Florida, miles of swamp, pine forest, and mosquitoes in the big bend of the state before you get round to the gulf beaches. There was a grinding noise beneath the van, but her mother had to keep driving, because there was no shoulder at all on the thin blacktop. She pulled into a little gas station built of cement blocks, the Aucilla River General Store. Out raced a man with a fire extinguisher. He was screaming and waving his hands, and he made her move the van away from the gas pumps.

> *... white sudsy stuff whooshing out, and I was still driving around, or trying to, with visions of movie fireball explosions going off in my mind, and thinking of Toots in the back sound asleep. Then I just hit the brakes and said enough of this, plucked up Toots in my arms, broke out of the van, and ran for dear life.*
>
> *Sure enough the van was on fire, at least the rear tires were. I was ten feet away and still running when the first tire blew—I thought it was the gas tank, and the next moment I was surprised to be still alive.*
>
> *I turned and watched the flames licking and black smoke just a-billowing out of the back of the van. I know I cried and hugged Toots way too tight. At the time I could not conceive of a worse disaster. In the van was everything we owned beyond the clothes on our backs. But months later I found myself dreaming that the or-*

nery beast, my albatross, had burned down to nothing there and then. It would have saved me a ton of heartbreak and my little bank account.

The fellow had emptied the extinguisher. Frantically he was yanking out a tangled garden hose. It didn't reach and he was swearing furiously until he saw I could hear him. But the extinguisher had taken the heart out of the flames, and things were just sort of smoldering and simmering down.

He gave up and came over to us wiping his brow, and running his hand over his bristly brush cut. Except for that stupid haircut he was quite a good-looking young guy—good chin and a kind face. He wore a camouflage T-shirt and tight jeans, I remember those real clear—why not—but most of all I recall the gun he had just a-dangling out of his back pocket. Only the barrel fit in (that's how tight the jeans were); the woodgrain handle sort of sashayed back and forth as he strutted about inspecting the damage.

He said his name was J J and I was terrified of the guy—with the haircut and that gun, he gave me a bad case of the jitters. And boy did he stare at me. It was hot and muggy and I wore a loose and I guess pretty filmy dress. That day Toots and I each had tiny flowers painted on our cheeks, but we could have been wearing fur loin-

cloths and nothing else save paper party hats and not gotten any more profound stares.

He was the first real live redneck I had ever met until we hit Texas, and even there he wouldn't have fallen second to none. He had more weapons than newspapers in his little store. I knew the gun in J J's back pocket was loaded and ready to pop. He told me so and proudly showed off how quick he could snap it out. Pow. Pow.

If a Greyhound bus had magically appeared at that moment I would have grabbed up Toots and just climbed aboard and fled that gas station cowboy, abandoned the van and everything. Philosophically we couldn't have been more opposed, and, as it became apparent, we were stuck there for a few days, I made a conscious decision to avoid discussing religion, or politics, or anything at all with him if I could. I was scared, and I kept my distance, and I realize now I was wrong.

While I puttered around inside the van sorting out the garbage—my big stock of candles had melted into one huge glob, which I found sort of funky and kept and ultimately used—J J settled Toots into his little one-room home in the back of the store and found some cartoons on the television. He started phoning old buddies. Pretty soon there was a redneck convention swarming all over, around and under my van. I tried to help, but finally J J told me to grab some beers out of the cooler for the boys and a soda for myself and the little girl—he always called Toots "the little girl." So I did.

I got a six-pack and went and looked in on Toots. I screamed. I became hysterical. I went ballistic. Grabbing her, I raced out. I sat her down in a swarm of bugs on an old wooden picnic table in front of the store, and I hugged her. I screamed and cried.

The boys stopped moving and stared at me like all their far-out suspicions were confirmed—I was beyond weird. J J ran over sort of scared-like and kept asking, "What happened? Y' okay? Y' okay?"

"Those guns," I sobbed, "they aren't loaded. Tell me they aren't." More than a dozen guns festooned the walls of the little back room where my daughter was watching Elmer Fudd hunting something, Bugs Bunny, probably, but I didn't wait around to catch the who or what.

" 'Course they're loaded. I've been robbed three times and shot at once. If I grab a gun, I ain't got no time to fool about loading her up."

I couldn't believe he'd just leave Toots alone with all those loaded guns, and I cried and kept screaming at him.

He looked supremely hurt; he was just trying to help me out. The boys in the background had

Death and Deception

wide eyes and open mouths. I could see it in their faces: "The poor hippie freak thinks guns are dangerous."

We had to stay parked beside the Aucilla River General Store for five days while the boys worked and worked hard on the van. J J was sort of the scariest man I had ever met, and also the politest—painfully polite—most generous, the kindest. If I was scared of him, he was terrified of me. He wouldn't take a penny for all the repairs, even forced some free groceries on us, acting for all the world like he was sorry for my misfortune, like the burned-up wheel bearing and ruined axle had somehow been his fault. I expect I unlearned more of the black-and-white misconceptions I possessed while sitting in the sticky heat swatting mosquitoes outside J J's little store than in any school or library. It was truly the bleakest place—worse than a flat desolate desert, a slum, or a gray northern metropolis; it had no redeeming qualities I could find—hot, muggy, buggy—uniformly boring pine trees everywhere blocking any sort of view. But for some reason real nice people chose to live there, and they even seemed to like it.

Madeline didn't remember this event. What she sort of hazily remembered was her mother talking, always chatting to people everywhere, and telling stories.

If she had to rely on her memory, Madeline wouldn't have had any strong reason to believe Anne Shannon was her mother, but she had the Polaroids. Could it be a coincidence that she had a faded black-and-white snapshot of a sooty Chevy van at a desolate Spur station, and another with pine trees and a group of good ol' boys grinning in front of the same van, now cleaned up, and that *Travels with Toots* had the good ol' boys and a fire and a stranded mother and daughter at a Spur station in bleak Aucilla River, Florida? How many blazing Chevy vans did J J get in the early seventies? How many young mom-and-daughter combinations lived for ten days at the Hiking Viking car dealership in Santa Maria, California, getting a new motor installed? That was in the book, and Madeline had a picture of her sitting under the hood in a vast empty engine cavity, a gaping wound where the van motor should normally be found.

There was more; each snapshot had its place somewhere in the book.

Madeline stared at those little snapshots. She must have more memories buried deep somewhere. But concentration didn't dig up any new thoughts. Unable to understand, too young to deal with her situation, she realized now she had long ago locked up that part of her mind.

She closed the file and left it on the kitchen table. Then she slipped on her jacket, put the little photo album in her pocket, and headed out. It was another slow-dawning day.

Chapter Eight

Madeline stood on the stoop and peered in through the window in the kitchen door. Steven was there, eyes down, watching the stream of coarse white grains tumble into the china sugar bowls, stopping when each was nearly full, then pausing and moving the scoop and funnel over to the next one in the row. He looked up as Madeline entered. His face was tired. Steven, who she thought could handle anything, was having trouble handling her sudden and inexplicable rejection. Madeline felt it even before their eyes met.

"Hi," she said softly. "Am I late?"

"No, not at all." His voice was louder than usual, with a bravado that faltered as he continued. "In fact, I wasn't even expecting you this morning. You should have slept in. You've got your big meeting today."

"I had trouble sleeping."

The easy smile was almost back. "Me too."

The big kitchen itself felt sleepy. Only one timer ticked. The counters were mostly clean and clear. Apparently the bike tour had gotten an early start and already left.

Steven unscrewed the lid of a tall wooden pepper mill.

"You okay?" Madeline asked.

"Just a bit tired."

"Steven, about last night..." she blurted out without thinking, wanting to say something that would explain everything and make things right and comfortable and warm again, but she didn't know what the right words were, and she was scared of the thoughts that came to mind. Her throat quickly dried; a simple swallow was a struggle.

The trickle of peppercorns stopped. It was Steven who finally broke the silence. His voice was soft and even. "Madeline, I want you to know that I could never hurt you."

Hurt her? She wasn't afraid of him. She was afraid of hurting him, afraid of losing his friendship.

"And I'd like to help. There are things going on here—" He interrupted himself, looking briskly away, then back again, before adding, "Things that I don't quite understand. But if you choose, you know, if you want to confide in me, well, I'll always be here for you." A few more peppercorns tumbled into the wooden mill.

Madeline looked at the floor. There'd been occasions in the past when she had desperately wanted to fall in love, to have someone special to share things with; she tried to, but couldn't. Sometimes she thought there might be something lacking in her, something wrong. Maybe she was incapable of love. Now, with Steven, she desperately did not want to fall in love, not anymore, but she couldn't stop herself. It was all she could do not to throw herself into his arms. *I can't love you, not really love you,* she wanted to cry out. *I'm your cousin.* But she couldn't, because then she would have to explain everything, and she just wasn't up to that, not yet. But she would, she would soon; she needed a little more time. Madeline felt frustration welling up inside her; she craved more work. She wanted to lose herself in frantic work. Where was a wedding reception or bus tour when you needed one?

It was the weakest smile she had ever seen him wear, but it was real and earnest, and unlike the many other smiles she had seen, this one tried valiantly to be happy, but faltered, and it hurt her to see it. She was hurting him, and she knew it. He tried to be as friendly as ever, but the sparkle in his eyes was weak. "I'm sorry," she said.

"You have no reason to be sorry. Never." He spoke so calmly and sincerely it was unequivocal—she had no reason to be sorry. "Whatever the problem, things will work out. They will." There was the smile growing again, albeit only a little, but that was enough to allow her the hope that somehow some miracle would occur and everything would work out okay.

Madeline half filled a saucepan with water before placing it on the burner. "Have you eaten?" she asked. "I can make you a soft-boiled egg if you'd like. We can use those egg cups."

He chuckled, soft and easy. "Okay. And we can sit out in the garden."

"Okay." She poured herself some grapefruit juice. "Any news on your father?"

He shook his head. "Not today, not yet. Mom will probably call soon."

An idea that had hovered in the dark recesses of her mind coalesced. With trepidation, Madeline asked, "Is she really your aunt, or do you just call her that, like an old family friend?"

"You mean Anne?" he asked with surprise.

"Yes."

"She's my aunt. My mother and she are sisters."

So much for that hope. Madeline fell away into her own thoughts. Did she really understand this entire cousin thing. She had wondered about that during the night. What were all those ancient Elvis Presley movies about—kissin' cousins?

"Not born here in Nova Scotia, though?" she stated, prodding him, as she put four slices of wholewheat bread in the toaster.

Steven had moved on to filling salt shakers. "No, my mom was born in Ontario—Toronto."

"Was your aunt born there as well?"

"Far as I know."

"Which sister is older?"

"My aunt."

Madeline slipped two eggs into the water. Anne Shannon was born in Toronto. She must have somehow adopted an American identity, Pamela Sue Paige. There were a couple of other things she wanted to confirm.

"Steven, does Anne have a dog?"

He was wiping his hands on a towel, then he looked at her, puzzled. "Raleigh?" he asked.

So there *was* a dog. Madeline turned on a timer and placed it on the shelf as she turned back to him. "Did she know where I was staying last night?"

"Yes. I think I did mention it to her. Why?"

"No reason."

"There must be a reason."

"I saw a dog nearby, that's all." Madeline shrugged, as though it wasn't anything important.

"A Great Dane? You can't miss Sir Walter Raleigh—he's as big as a horse."

"Really?"

"Well, almost. But he's a pussycat. Exceptionally well trained."

"That's good to know."

"He could maul you to death with love though."

While they ate they discussed the finicky nature of soft-boiled eggs, and the simple secrets of croissants; they talked of flower names and favorite blossoms, the smell of black earth and gardening, the dew and the way every morning the sun slowly burned off the morning haze; the bay, sailing, travel; they touched just a little on politics, but each avoided any mention of the subject most on their minds. It was a pleasant breakfast, a fun breakfast, and at times an awkward breakfast, especially as Madeline found herself being drawn closer and closer into the warmth of his love.

"I've got to get going," Steven said as he stood and stacked the empty dishes on the tray. "I'm running a few errands in town."

"Should I stay here, in case anyone wants to check in, or out, or anything?"

"No. Nothing is going to happen. Lois can handle the place." Lois was ghostlike. She sailed through the building, cleaned the rooms, and mysteriously only appeared when needed. She'd been doing the job for almost twenty years and was as much a fixture as the front desk or the fireplace.

"So what should I do?"

"Relax. Get ready for your meeting. I'll be back by lunch."

"I could cut some flowers—"

"We have rooms filled with fresh flowers and at the moment, no guests."

"Maybe I could do some weeding in the garden, or

something." Digging her hands into damp black earth appealed to her.

"Sure, if you'd like, but you should take the opportunity to take it easy. I've got to take the rubbish to the dump, hit the bank, a few other things, all boring, or else I'd show you around, take you for a sail or something. Maybe later we can. And don't worry, we'll be busy again. It's the nature of this business—feast or famine, then you can work to your heart's content. Relax."

"I can't relax."

He looked at her with surprise. "Hmm, it's good to know I'm not the only one." The tension continued, almost pulsating in the air between them. Then Steven added with wry humor, "But we have to try our best, until we get these things sorted out."

"I need something to do." She had a couple of hours to kill before meeting Anne. She wanted to work.

"Get a book from our little library on the first floor landing or try a walk on the beach. There is nothing more relaxing than a walk on the beach."

Madeline forced herself to sit in the split-log chair on the front deck of her little cabin. She tried again to read. She'd found the history of the Harbourview Colony and managed to read all the way to where Anne Shannon and her longtime friend Lois Trent had arrived, Anne to the stone cottage, Lois to a small home on the road into town; Anne to work on her book, Lois to her job as a cleaning woman.

High out in the wispy faint haze above the bay a herring gull complained. The tide was out and the small rocks were smooth and slick. Two pickup trucks had driven out onto the tidal flats and men were harvesting clams, tossing back the stones and raking the exposed black muck. There was no wind at all. Still, the water was moving, alive, undulating like it was panting trying to catch its breath. Something about staring at vast pools of moving water was good for the soul, like a massage for the weary muscle of the mind. However, she still suffered a surging wave of anxiety; she was shuddering with fear. There was more than an hour to kill, and she had no work to do.

In a moment Madeline was up and pacing again. She wandered through the little cottage until she ended up in the washroom. Brushing her hair, she stared critically into the mirror. There wasn't much she could do with hair so short. She washed again. She brushed her teeth. There was nothing else to do. She continued to stare into the mirror. *There is nothing wrong with me; there is no reason for Anne Shannon to reject me out of hand. There is nothing wrong with me,* she repeated. It was silly to think this way, but she couldn't help it.

Unable to wait any longer, Madeline walked the long way around to the stone cottage and kept walking all the way to the end of the cottage road. She wandered into the meadow and around the empty chapel, up the aisle to the little pulpit and back to the pews. She sat down, stood up, and wandered outside. Checking her watch, she was still twenty minutes early and wondering what to do when she realized she was being watched. Across the road, across the yard, Anne Shannon stood in the doorway of the stone cottage. She stared directly at Madeline. At that point it seemed ridiculous for Madeline to do anything other than go to her. So she did, walking along the lane, not speaking, not knowing whether to smile or not, turning onto the path of white limestone tablets laid deep in the thick grass.

Chapter Nine

She forced herself to speak. "Good morning." The voice was more strident than she had intended; it sounded challenging and she didn't want to sound challenging, but she was afraid of appearing weak as well. Madeline dropped her head and walked up the three wooden steps to the veranda.

Anne remained standing in the open doorway. She made no move to invite Madeline in.

"Thank you for seeing me," Madeline continued.

The older woman nodded warily, and then she began to speak, coolly perhaps, but not coldly. "I want to apologize," Anne said. "The other day, I'm afraid you caught me at a bad time."

"My fault. I'm sure I startled you. Just appearing like that on your veranda. I'm sorry." Madeline's voice began to falter but she dove in with determination. "First of all my name isn't really Madeline Paige."

This caught the older woman's interest, but only for an instant.

"It *was* Madeline Paige, but my mother disappeared when I was young, and I was adopted, so now it's Madeline Rosetti. I said Paige the other day, in case you knew the name," she said before adding softly, "in case you knew my mother."

The woman did not respond in any way.

"Did you know her?"

The pause was long but it didn't feel like the woman was working at remembering. "I don't believe so."

Madeline had intended to begin with small talk, establish some rapport. At the best of times, she had trouble making small talk. Finagling with a computer didn't create the gift of gab; she tried, but often felt clumsy in social situations.

"It's a beautiful home you have."

"Thank you."

"You've lived here a long time. I understand it used to be a wealthy sea captain's home, well over a hundred years old, built even before the inn or the other cottages."

"That's almost right. Captain Westacott was lost at sea. His wife came here and had this cottage built, and the inn, the chapel, and the first gardens."

They still stood on the front veranda. Anne blocked

the doorway, holding the screen door open. When working her way through college, Madeline had briefly gone door to door trying to sell household products, cleaners, and cosmetics; the feeling was the same, like she was imposing on a stranger, and only good manners forced the stranger to tolerate her presence, alert for the first opportunity to end the sham.

"I recently read your book. I loved it. It reminded me of a trip I took with my mother around the same—"

Anne snapped, "I don't discuss the book."

"Why?" Madeline asked. "It's terrific. Very powerful, and warm and insightful."

"It's old news; it's in the past." A tense and stony look was fixed on Anne's face.

"Are you working on a new book?"

"I'd prefer not to speak of my work at all. Or my personal life." And there was no indication the cold-eyed woman blocking the doorway would ever move or consent to speak again.

"Steven says you don't travel anymore."

Anne gave a minute shake of her head, no.

"Why?" Madeline waited for a response. Her skin was hot and prickly. She was working hard to remain calm and congenial. This was worse than any college exam. She felt lost, cautiously feeling her way.

Finally Anne spoke. "I've traveled enough. I like it here."

"It *is* very nice, very peaceful," Madeline agreed

with a weak smile. "You must have traveled a lot before you wrote the book. Steven says you lived in quite a few different places."

There was no response.

"You worked in New York? What did you do?"

"A lot of dull little jobs."

"Was that difficult? Being a Canadian, didn't you need a special permit, a green card?"

"That's the past."

"Oh." Madeline thought for a moment. "Is your new book fiction, or—"

"I don't believe that's any of your business."

"But you agreed to speak to me."

"Only because Stevie asked me to. He said it was very important for him."

Madeline was beginning to panic. The interview would end very soon unless she could find something to talk about. "But this isn't seeing me. You won't talk. You have to say something." A pleading tone had crept into Madeline's voice; she fought it off. "You aren't even going to invite me in, are you?"

Anne hesitated a moment then moved back into the front hall.

It took courage for Madeline to enter the house, but courage she had; in fact it was something she always possessed, and right then her trembling anger gave her even more. It was a struggle to remain calm. She commented on the house. The windowpanes in the front door were cut glass with flowers etched in the corners.

There was dark solid-wood wainscoting in the large entry hall and the same wood formed a heavy trim and eyebrows in the formal dining room to the left. To the right Madeline glimpsed a sitting room, but the staircase captivated her attention. Rising up from the hall, it began very wide, tapering and turning gently as it rose, with heavy wooden balustrades. Built into the walls were dark wood bookcases, floor to ceiling, brightly varnished, and the banister melded into the structure. At the top of the stairs was a dormer with a large window that allowed a beam of sunlight to bathe the stairway, books, and bookcases.

"It's beautiful," Madeline murmured in awe. It was almost a shrine to books.

"Thank you."

"You must love books." She ran her hand along the banister and read titles: mainly classics, the great works of literature, many old and leather bound, very many she had never heard of.

"Yes," Anne concurred as she led Madeline into the sitting room. "I've always loved books." Here the wood was also dark in tone, the furniture was antique, everything was painfully neat—lace doilies, crystal vases with fresh flowers, original oil paintings: seascapes mostly, with ornate frames. And there was no sign of the dog. In fact it was hard to imagine such a huge beast ever being in the room without innocently destroying things.

Madeline sat on the chesterfield across from the armchair that Anne occupied.

"It's all very lovely, your home, the antiques. The wood is so beautiful. I've never seen wood like it."

"Thank you. I find wood enchanting, especially old wood; it seems to become more intriguing with age. Like the sea—I can gaze upon it for hours."

"Yes," Madeline agreed eagerly, pleased that her mother had finally started to open up to her, but already she saw the cloak of distance being drawn back down. "This trip has been a revelation to me," she said. "The water, and the flowers are so beautiful. I'm from California, which is much warmer and drier, also beautiful but entirely different. Well, I don't have to tell you about California; you've been there, of course."

The older woman nodded, but the indication was she wasn't interested.

"That's where your book ends."

Anne was determined to be cold. She said nothing.

Madeline was becoming impatient. "I'm afraid I've never traveled much, not since I was small." It was a harsh silence that followed. "Did you make the trip that's related in the book? Or is it fiction?"

Anne could have been a statue for all the reaction she displayed. Madeline rose out of her seat. Her frustration surged; she couldn't sit still. "Why can't you talk about the book? I don't understand. Aren't you proud of it?" Madeline was starting to tremble again.

Anne was in no hurry to respond. Her eyes narrowed and inspected Madeline closely. "It's mostly fiction," Anne finally stated. "I've been to many of the places in the book, heard stories about others, made some up. It's mostly fiction."

Madeline pressed on. "And the daughter in the book? What happened to your daughter?"

"Of course, there never was a daughter." The older woman closed her eyes and looked away to the front hall, the stairs, the books. "That part was complete fiction. I classified the book as 'faction,' a blend of fact and fiction. The publisher thought it would be more successful as a travel adventure, so they discounted the fictional aspects."

Madeline sat back down, resting only on the edge of the chair. "So why have a daughter in it at all then?"

"Because nothing pries open cold hearts like a pretty little three-year-old girl; everyone loves a child, a laughing little girl. It's the best way to travel. People are friendly; they're not after anything, you meet their best side. A story about a trip by a single woman in her mid-twenties would be quite a different adventure, wouldn't it?"

She made a child sound like an indispensable part of a traveler's equipment—camera, passport, change of clothing, a three-year-old girl with curly gold hair.

"I see. And were J J and the Aucilla River store fact or fiction?"

"I've already said more than I should. I really don't talk about the book."

"But I found J J such an interesting character. Is he real? He was; he must be. And that little store in that swampy pine forest. Most people think Florida is all glitzy but you showed a very different side, a human side of it."

While Madeline had been speaking, Anne had begun to slowly shake her head. Then she stood, head still shaking, and walked away to the sliding glass doors overlooking the bay.

Madeline followed her into the dining room. "I don't understand why you don't like to talk about it. You love books. I mean, the bookcase and all those wonderful books you have..."

Anne continued to stare at the water, but a small light had been kindled deep in the blackness of her eyes. She murmured low, slow, and trancelike, "Yes. Yes, I do love books. I used to think that to have written a book, even just one small book, was the highest achievement a woman could aspire to."

"Used to think? You don't think that anymore?"

Anne was lost in the haze of her own thoughts, and for a moment Madeline wondered if she had even heard the question.

"Writing a book..." she began, and stumbled on her words. "Writing a book, that is the highest achievement possible, truly."

Madeline's excitement caused her to miss the slight

differences in the two statements. "And your wonderful book, you must be very proud of it. It was critically acclaimed, and very successful, and very good."

Anne's eyes fell away from the bay and seemed to focus only on the empty air inches before her face.

"Tell me about J J," Madeline prodded gently. "He was real, wasn't he?"

Anne didn't speak.

"That little store and the fire?"

She didn't respond at all.

"The little girl and those guns?" Madeline reached into her jacket pocket. Out came the small wallet. She opened it, first to the picture of herself in front of the derelict van, then J J and the boys.

Anne swung her glassy stare around to fall upon the picture. Her eyes widened.

Madeline flipped back to the beginning, then slowly cycled through each picture. She commented on them as they passed, using names and phrases taken directly from the book. She finished and closed the book. She tried to find Anne's eyes. They'd gone blank, like they had seen too much and couldn't take any more in.

"You know who I am, don't you?" Madeline asked softly.

Finally Anne moved. She raised one hand and grasped the handle of the glass door. At first she didn't have the strength to yank it open. Madeline helped. The door slipped open. Anne began to step outside and stopped, allowing Madeline to go first. Madeline stepped out into the sun and the gentle breeze. The fresh air made her labored breathing easier.

She turned back to Anne, waiting for her. "You know who I am, don't you?"

Anne didn't follow her out onto the front veranda. "Yes," she murmured. "Madeline Paige... Rosetti. Madeline Rosetti. I have a good memory."

"How good? There really was a daughter, wasn't there? This girl here in the picture. Me."

Again there was the icy silence and the same impervious gaze. Anne was only middle-aged, not old, but she was weak and tired. Still, the challenge in Madeline's voice rekindled her ire and her strength. Saying nothing, she slid shut the door between them. She flicked the lock.

"Why?" Madeline pleaded. Her hand became a fist and she just managed to stop herself from pounding on the glass. "Don't you think I have a right to know? You know who I am, you do. I'm the daughter, aren't I?" There, it was out in the open, and Anne Shannon didn't seem surprised at all—she knew. The older woman was not angry, more sad than anything.

"I don't want money or anything. I just want to know. I don't understand. Why, why are you doing this? You seem to be suffering more than I am. Here you are in this beautiful home, with your wonderful books to comfort you—very few people in the world have anything like that, and you are alone, cold and miserable. At least that's the way it seems to me. Why? You don't have to be so unhappy.''

Anne Shannon turned away as if there was no one there.

Madeline was dumbfounded. She hadn't thought it possible, but again the incredible gall of the woman had shocked her. The situation was truly hopeless. The total and complete rejection by her mother was enough to drive her away. After all, she had the makings of a comfortable life back in San Jose, a nice apartment and a promising career; she liked her work. Still, it would always be painful to know her mother was alive, yet disinterested. And to think of Steven, to be near him, was just as bad. There was nothing but sadness here for her. She felt confident she knew the truth. All that was left to do was gather up her belongings and say good-bye to Steven.

She was still on the veranda, but it was time to go. The soothing pulse of the water drew her and she fled to the front yard intending to head down to the beach. Halfway across the lawn there was a new sound, a scuffling—a torrent of thuds. Madeline stopped to listen. Almost instantly she knew what it was. A moment later there was a flash of tan bounding around the corner from the front of the house. Raleigh, she realized. He was still yards away, and she held out her hands to him, palms up, in a friendly gesture. She tried to stare him down; she tried to stand her ground. But the dog didn't care; he galloped toward her. There was a low growl. The key with dogs, she knew, was to be friendly and show no fear. Steven had said he was a pussycat, but this pussycat was huge with huge teeth and huge paws and claws, and he galloped like a horse, and the horse was coming straight at her. Madeline flinched. She turned and fled, across the lawn and down the steps. No time was wasted looking back. Sliding and stumbling over the slick rocks, she reached the water and carried on, ready to try swimming, but the coolness oozed through her shoes and that caused her to hesitate. She glanced back. The dog had stopped at the top of the stairs. He snuffled at her but showed no inclination to continue his pursuit. She was terrified of dogs, especially big gangly beasts, and she was tired and trembling as she hurried further away. The dog stared, mouth dangling open, watching her as he paced back and forth, gouging shreds of wood out of the steps with his claws.

Chapter Ten

Steven drew the dinghy alongside the slender wooden sloop. He shipped the oars and stood and reached out to grab hold of the boat by the bulwarks. The deck was white and the topsides dark blue. Painted on the transom in gold leaf was the name *True Blue*. The boat was modest but well-found, clean, and orderly.

Saying good-bye hadn't been as easy as she had expected. Madeline had packed, and then tried writing a note for Steven. She took out her pad and flipped past her notes on Anne Shannon, but before she had found suitable words, he was there at her cabin door with a large wicker basket, an invitation to go sailing, and the shy and friendly smile. "No" was the right thing to say, and "I'm leaving," and the truth—she should have told him the whole truth, right then, and she wanted to. But where to start? What to say? How should she say it? What would his reaction be? Madeline tossed her notepad onto the kitchen counter and then pushed it further into the corner, behind the refrigerator. It was wrong to put off the moment, but it was easier, and at that moment she was feeling weak, and not at all sure she had the strength to say goodbye.

True Blue heeled slightly to one side as Madeline boarded.

"Don't worry, she won't tip." He pushed the basket up on deck, then added in a mumble just loud enough for her to hear, "I hope."

Madeline sat in the cockpit feeling awkward and wondering what she could do to help. She'd never been on a small boat before. The dinghy had felt precarious; the slender sailboat was substantially bigger but it felt even tippier.

Steven pulled the dinghy hand over hand forward, to the bow, and called back, "You can swim, right?"

"A little."

He had tied the dinghy to the mooring and swung himself up onto the bow. "Great. Not that it matters much; the water is so cold we wouldn't last long anyway."

"Great," she answered, and she drew the word out long and slow.

He stopped peeling back the blue cover from the sail and looked at her and laughed.

"Okay, so what do I do?" Madeline asked.

"Take the tiller and steer," he said.

"I don't know how."

"Don't worry, you will in a moment."

"But—"

"Would you rather raise and set the sails?"

"I don't know—"

He interrupted her with a shrug and a smile.

Madeline suddenly looked up to find the boats moored nearby were on the move, yet there was nobody on board. And the shoreline was slipping away. "Hey!" With a start she realized *True Blue* was the one in motion. "We're moving!"

He continued to smile. "Just with the tide." Already he had started to hoist the mainsail and the edges of the light canvas were beginning to flutter in the breeze.

She was amazed at how fast they were going with just the tide and the river current speeding them along. Now the sail was snapping, and the boom was gyrating angrily as Steven stood before the mast and finished hauling it up into the air. He jumped to the side deck and then into the cockpit beside her. He grabbed the tail of a rope.

"It's noisy."

"Just a second." He gave the rope another tug and the boom shut up and the sail became as smooth and quiet as the skin on a drum. The boat tipped to one side and accelerated. The hairs on the back of her neck stood up. Unaware of what to do, she just clenched tight the tiller.

"So." There was nervousness in her voice and she paused to reassert control. "Have you ever tipped over this boat?"

"Capsized? 'Course not." He was back on the deck and walking away from her. "A boat like this you can pretty well capsize only once." There was that sparkle in his eyes again.

"Why?" The question was a nervous reflex.

"Because it will sink."

"Great," she said again, drawing out the word. "Sink," she added with a nod. A splendid way to end a splendid day, she mused.

"Like a rock. Water rushes into the cabin, fills it up, down she goes. Capsizing is not a good idea." He was bent away from her, working on the lines, so she couldn't see his face, but she could hear the smile in his voice. "Don't worry, there is a half a ton of lead in the keel. So the bottom is happy to stay down, which keeps the top up and the water out. This boat doesn't want to tip over."

"Good."

"It's much more likely we'll hit a rock, rip a hole in the bottom, and sink that way. There are quite a lot of treacherous reefs out here, and quite a few wrecks scattered across the bottom."

"Great. And you want me to steer?" She held the tiller tightly but didn't dare move it. "What do I do?"

"It's easy. Just don't hit any of the rocks."

Madeline glanced around. That seemed easy enough. "Where are the rocks?"

"You can't see them because they are under the water."

"But—"

"Well, depending on the state of the tide, they are usually underwater. The tides here are about fifteen feet. Out on the bay they reach the high thirties, highest in the world. So sometimes the rocks are deep underwater and sometimes just below the surface, sometimes above."

"Wonderful."

"See that red buoy?"

"No."

Steven was back beside her and he placed his hand atop hers on the slender ash tiller. Pulling it back and forth, he showed her how the boat quickly reacted to any movement.

"Aim the bow just to the right of it."

"I don't know how—"

"I'll be right back; you're doing great. Don't worry—if anything goes wrong, I'll scream at you."

"Thanks, I appreciate that."

So far Madeline had done nothing but clutch the long wooden tiller. Watching him nimbly move down the side deck to the very pinnacle of the bow, she decided she had better figure out this entire steering thing. She started by yanking the tiller toward her. After all, there were only two things she could do, pull it toward her or push it away. She could feel water pressure rapidly build as she pulled. The boat began to twirl the opposite way to what she expected. Next she thrust the tiller away and the boat rocked and spun back. It seemed simple enough. She rocked it back and forth some more, getting the feel of things. It was surprising how quickly and dramatically the boat reacted to her adjustments. She watched the shore as she swung the boat back and forth, back and forth. Then, looking up, she saw Steven staring at her. He was clenching the wire forestay and holding tight, not moving, no longer working, a mix of surprise and terror upon his face.

"You know, I think I've got it. Steering is sort of fun," Madeline hollered with a large smile.

"Yes, well, I'm glad you are enjoying yourself. Perhaps we should review the man overboard procedure."

His laughter brought light into her eyes.

A minute tug or nudge, Madeline discovered, was all it took to wiggle the nose of the boat and line it up where she wanted to go—just to the right of the red buoy.

Again a sail began to flap and snap. The big genoa was up and bitterly complaining. Steven jogged down the side deck. Quickly he was at her side, hauling in the sheet that controlled the snapping sail.

"Keep steering," he muttered before grunting as he pulled and tamed the genoa. Again the sail became quiet; the only sound now was the swift rush and gurgle of the water streaming along the hull.

She missed hitting the buoy by less than a foot, skimming by close enough to see the bird droppings and the welds beneath the rust and the red paint, close enough to touch. "Now where?" Madeline asked, finally releasing her concentration from the red channel marker and looking at Steven.

He was cringing, slowly opening his eyes. He took a breath before saying, "M-m-maybe next time we shouldn't cut it so fine. Stay between the red and green, and try to avoid the fishing boat up ahead. M-m-maybe by more than a few inches."

"Oh." Madeline pouted, but her eyes were wild and playful. "You know, I'm trying my best."

"And you're doing great." Then he added, "Really great," and again he expanded the length of the word great.

He sat on the bridge deck before her, reached back through the companionway, and grabbed the wicker basket. He set out sandwiches and a cheese plate and poured wine into plastic glasses.

"Okay, now that you've fallen into my trap and you can't get away, tell me all about your meeting this morning." There was something serious in his demeanor but nothing sinister. "What happened?"

Madeline shrugged her shoulders. She ate with one

hand and continued to steer with the other. She was glad she had something to do, glad for a reason to look away from him to the wind, the waves, and the channel markers. She studied the froth of white water gurgling over the smooth, bald rocks that had poked their heads out above the surface and the scattered patches of golden brown indicating reefs were lurking just below. "The woman hates me."

"Not possible."

"Oh, it's more than possible. It's a fact."

"Why would she hate you?"

Again Madeline shrugged her shoulders.

"Maybe it will just take time."

"No. There is no more time. I've given up."

"I can't believe that. You're not the type."

Steven didn't realize how devastating the morning had been for her. Of course he didn't realize, she chided herself. In his eyes Madeline had just been rejected by a cantankerous author who didn't want to discuss her book. Of course he suspected there was more to it, but he couldn't have dreamed that Madeline had been rejected by her own mother. Somehow, she would have to find the courage to tell him.

They had long passed the little aluminum fishing boat and were moving farther out into the ever-widening bay. The wind was fresher here, and the boat eagerly leaped from wave to wave. The bow reared up and crashed into a large foamy white crest; they were doused with spray. Madeline wiped her hand across her wet face. She tasted the salt on her lips. "Did I do something wrong?"

"No, just a freak wave. We're getting out into open water, that's all." He collected the lunch leftovers and secured them in the basket before dropping everything onto the cuddy cabin. Then he slid the companionway hatch closed and fastened the hasp.

"Are we in any danger?" She knew nothing of sailing, but it seemed like the gentle glide she had enjoyed was becoming violent.

"No," he scoffed. "Not at all. This is great sailing weather."

The word "great" seemed to mean a lot of different and contrasting things to him, and she knew she had started on the same habit.

Whether sailing was dangerous or not, she didn't know. It felt dangerous, but never before had danger thrilled her.

"Should I be afraid?"

"Of course not."

"Then I'm not. I trust you."

"But not enough . . ." he started. There was a slight weight to his words, a somberness, a hint of sadness. ". . . to tell me what's really going on."

The bow continued to rear up and slam down into the white froth. The boat responded with eerie creaks and groans.

Steven's eyes were caring. Would *not* telling him cost her his love? What to say, how to say it? She knew she'd cry and be unable to stop. If she started, she knew the words would gush out—they were a bursting, tangled knot in the pit of her stomach—and she'd become a sorry, sobbing, weak, and unwanted woman with a selfish tale of woe. Tell, don't tell; no choice appeared to be the right choice.

Reluctantly, Steven continued. "It's okay. Anytime you want to talk..." Enough said, he allowed the thought to drift away on the breeze.

Here was her opportunity, she realized. In a moment she could explain everything, but then she was certain he would look at her differently. She'd no longer be the strong, independent career woman. She'd be an unwanted, unloved, abandoned child. His respect would be colored with pity. She didn't want that; she wanted them to be equals.

Another heavy wave rolled the boat and Steven used the motion to rock to his feet. "Time to tack," he announced. He gave her a new point to aim for, this time back up in the shelter of the river mouth, and as she turned the boat around he popped ropes out of cam cleats and drew others in snug. The boat rolled over from one side to the other, then hanging in the air on its new cant, it quieted, steadied, and began to lunge forward once more.

The breeze was in their teeth now and whipping their hair. "The wind is a lot stronger?" she asked.

Steven quickly explained how they had been traveling with the wind, which was the easiest point of sailing—there was a saying among sailors that a haystack can sail downwind. "This feels faster but it isn't. If the breeze is twenty knots and the boat is going about five, then the wind feels like we're doing about fifteen when we are going with the wind and about twenty-five when we are beating into it. That's the real difference."

"Is there going to be a test on this when we get back?" she asked trying to be glib, but whether it was the challenging sea conditions or her refusal to confide in him, the sense of levity was gone.

The pressures on the rudder were much stronger and she struggled to hold on. Steven moved in beside her. He took the tiller. His body blocked the breeze and the spray, and she felt warmer nestled in close to him.

"You're not just another fan of her book, are you?" he said matter-of-factly. There was no playfulness in his voice. He didn't look at her, still watching the sails and the bow of the dancing boat.

Madeline didn't dare look at him. She stared blankly at his strong hand gripping the tiller, making minor adjustments in response to the bash of each wave.

"Madeline, I've changed my mind. I'm not going to wait for you to tell me. I've been patient, I am patient, but . . . You are obsessed with my aunt."

She bit the inside of her cheek. She must tell him.

He spoke very slowly. "I've thought a lot about the

book and Anne and you. You think you're Toots. Am I right?''

Still biting her cheek, she nodded, glanced up, and found herself caught in the beam of his eyes. He was smiling, soft and comfortable—it was his "we can manage this, everything is going to be okay" smile. He looped one foot over the tiller and leaned back. An arm slipped around her shoulders; he hugged her.

Madeline opened her mouth and began to speak. The dam burst. The words flooded out. She didn't stop until she had told him everything she knew. The unburdening felt wonderful, but even to her the proof of her suspicions sounded weak and confusing. She wished she had her notebook and snapshots with her; beyond her sketchy memories, that was her most conclusive proof.

"And it's definitely you in those pictures?"

"Yes, I think so. I can't imagine who else it could be, or why I would have them if it wasn't me, and they sort of look like me. So . . ."

"I'd like to see them."

"When we get back."

"You've always had them?"

"Yes, they were in the van when my mother went missing. They gave them to me—I don't remember whom, the police I guess or some authorities—but I kept them. I didn't have much. There was also a tattered notebook of poetry, but it sort of disintegrated."

The boat skimmed past the red buoy. Closer to

shore the water flattened; gradually the boat ceased to leap about. Still it kept driving forward.

"That would make us cousins. And that is why you suddenly changed your attitude toward me."

"My attitude never changed; it just became impossible for us to have"—she paused, feeling self-conscious—"that kind of relationship."

"Yes, I see. But you aren't my cousin."

Madeline was taken aback by the words and the simple way he stated them, like it was an obvious fact.

"You see, I have a large number of cousins." He gave her back the tiller and stood and looked full at her. "In fact, some very nice cousins; you'll like them. But I don't feel about them what I feel for you." He moved up onto the deck and walked toward the mast. With Steven around it was easy to believe anything was possible.

He called out, "I hope you don't mind if I do a little investigating. Because we aren't cousins and Auntie Anne isn't your mother." The mainsail began to skitter down. White cloth fluttered and fell across the cabin top.

"How do you know?"

"If we're not cousins, she can't be."

"But...she must be. There is no other explanation."

"There is. We just haven't thought of it yet." He was gathering up the material and folding it along the boom. He stopped. "You know, I think we are going about this all wrong. We have to try to be logical. Remember, it's not just you Anne avoids talking to, it's everyone.''

"So?"

"I don't know. I'm just thinking out loud, and it doesn't make sense to me.'' He was concentrating. ''She's been hiding something for years, don't you think? Why else would she be so secretive?''

"I guess because it's against the law to fake your own death.''

"I don't know much about the law, but after all this time . . . I mean, isn't there a statute of limitations, or something? Couldn't she work out some sort of deal? Wouldn't *anything* be worth it if you gained a daughter in the bargain?''

"Obviously she doesn't feel that way.''

"Come now, no one is that crazy, not even Auntie Anne.'' He stood at the bow and told her to go past the mooring buoy.

The little harbor looked different. New rocks protruded from the watery depths. Ashore the beach was wider than she had seen it before.

"The tide has changed, so turn hard now, right around, and aim straight back for the buoy.'' Madeline did. The boat coasted to a stop. Steven lay on the deck and reached down and grabbed the mooring line. "Great,'' he said, and this time there wasn't a hint of ambiguity. Then he stood back up and said, "She isn't your mother. I don't know if that makes you happy or sad, but she isn't your mother. She can't be, can she? She doesn't act like any mother I've ever known or heard of."

Madeline was tempted to enlighten him here, her childhood experiences being considerably different from his, but she remained silent.

"We're going to see her tonight, okay? We can handle this." And of course there was the comforting hint of a smile in his eyes. It almost made her believe everything would be all right.

Chapter Eleven

The notepad wasn't there, not where she'd left it. As Madeline picked up the kettle, she stared into the empty corner by the refrigerator. Her notepad should be there . . . shouldn't it? A chill began to wriggle up into the bones of her shoulders. She had to be mistaken. She had pushed the pad deep into the corner when Steven arrived, concealing it from him; she remembered doing it, clearly she remembered doing it and feeling guilty. Now it all seemed quite silly; now she was eager to show him her notes and pictures, but the pad wasn't there and that was distressing. She could see it in her mind's eye, sliding into the corner, and she couldn't remember moving it after that.

Turning on the stove, she ran the tap and filled the kettle, looking again along the counter. It wasn't there and it hadn't fallen down the crack beside the refrigerator, but as she stood and placed the kettle on the burner, she turned slightly and caught sight of the pad sitting out plainly on the kitchen table. For an instant Madeline was relieved, but only for an instant. She was almost certain she hadn't put it there. Lois? Had Lois been in to clean up? There were no other signs that someone had been in. It was perplexing. She concluded she must have moved it herself and just forgotten.

Walking into the bedroom, Madeline peeled off her damp sweatshirt. She was eager for Steven to see her notes and the little photo album. It felt surprisingly good to have someone she trusted share her burden. She hung her jeans on the door. With one outfit salty and wet, she didn't have much choice of what to wear; only one clean blouse was left and one more wearing had to be squeezed out of her cords. If she stayed any longer she'd have to do a wash, better yet, go shopping. Just to get home now she'd have to do something.

The kettle was starting to boil so she went back and poured the water into the little teapot, grabbed a cup and an oatmeal-raisin cookie, and sat down. Flipping through her two pages of notes, Madeline again wondered if her mind was playing tricks on her. She was quite certain she had tossed the pad onto the kitchen counter, and couldn't remember touching it after that.

Turning to the first blank page, she began to add a new note.

Anne Shannon contends Toots was fictitious, as was most of the book. She had only visited some of the locations where the book . . .

Madeline stopped in mid-sentence. She got a pencil from her knapsack. She turned the pencil on its side and began to shade the page. Then she stopped and held the page up to the light. She squinted. It was difficult to make out. There was the imprint of her own notes; she tended to have a heavy hand and the ballpoint pen she used left distinct marks, but there was more. She walked out onto the deck and into the sunlight. She angled the paper. While Madeline usually printed in block letters, probably due to her years of writing out computer code, someone in a fluid hand had written *Mother born Pamela Sue Paige, May 24, 1947, in Syracuse, New York.*

Someone had made a copy of her notes! In fact, it looked like they had copied out everything, then torn away the page. Someone had been in the little cottage, seen her notepad, and copied it. Who? Why?

Anne, she wondered, or maybe Steven? That morning, she had been with Anne, so Steven had an opportunity and a key, and had known her whereabouts, and that afternoon while sailing he had announced he suspected she thought she was Toots. Had he figured that out, or read it in her notebook? But she didn't believe he could possibly do something like that. The only real suspect was Anne. When she was out sailing with Steven, Anne had her opportunity to snoop, but surely Anne already knew the details. She didn't need to make a copy. Why would she want to make a copy of the notes?

Madeline sank into the rough log chair on the deck, where she sat with her feet up on the middle rung of the railing and listened to the sounds that made up the silence. Cradled in her hands was the lukewarm teacup. The afternoon breeze was dying. The sun was swelling big and red and slipping into the treetops. There was a pattern to the summer weather: the cool morning mist, the hot sun breaking through before noon. Then the clouds would evaporate and an onshore breeze would build up with the warmth of the day. The nights began warm and clear, then rapidly cooled, and the moon would begin to disappear first in a fuzzy halo, then in a thick cottony white blanket that seemed to grow up out of the wet grass.

Steven had given her hope. Anne Shannon couldn't possibly be her mother—why would she need to make a copy of those simple facts? Didn't she know already? Her mother would know. She was more confused than ever. Maybe her mother had drowned years ago. Maybe she wasn't destined to regain a mother; that was sad, but then maybe nothing was preventing her from establishing a relationship with Steven.

When Madeline had stumbled upon the book, at first she was surprised someone had taken a trip so similar to hers. As she read, she hadn't clearly remembered the scenes in the book—it was many years ago and she had only been three and four at the time. But she did have the pictures, and they did coincide closely with the book's events. Could the similarities between her trip and the book just have been a strange coincidence?

What she sort of remembered was her mother telling and retelling the stories. No, that wasn't quite right; it wasn't the stories she remembered so much as it was the endless waiting, the hot, dry car dealership waiting rooms, the uncomfortable plastic chairs, the flickering television doling out dull daytime game shows, and all the somber people, quiet, leafing through tattered magazines, not looking at one another. Strange as it seemed, the clearest memory Madeline had was of glittering specks of dust floating in the bright sunbeams that streamed in through the windows. To this day, seeing dust specks floating in the air, glinting in the sunlight, brought back the vivid memory of waiting rooms, and playing with broken toys on a thinly carpeted floor, bored, while in the background her mother would chat away. Her mother would laugh and regale the nameless, faceless strangers with tales of travel and misfortune: the camper catching fire and the two rear tires exploding, J J and his guns and tight jeans, the two front tires disintegrating moments apart in the worst of the west Texas wastelands, or the transmission quitting high in the mountains of California (her mother had to peer into the side view mirrors as the van freewheeled backward down a steep and winding highway). It wasn't really the actual details of the stories that Madeline remembered. She remembered following the slow drift of the sparkling dust particles and waving her hands to stir the air and make them dance, and in the background her mother would be laughing and telling and retelling stories and people would be listening.

According to the book, they once spent ten days hanging around a Chevy dealer in Santa Maria, California, the car repair taking the last of their savings, so they had nothing to do but wait. At night the dealer pushed the car out into the back lot and they slept in it, eating meals like spaghetti with a noxious sauce made from little packets of ketchup and mustard filched from a McDonald's restaurant a block away. The van's motor was shot, largely because they had sprung an oil leak in El Paso, Texas. They asked a Chevy dealer to fix the leak, and he did, replacing a blown head gasket, but they hadn't specifically asked him to replace the leaked-away oil and he hadn't. So they headed off into the mountains of New Mexico with an engine that didn't have any oil. Strange as it sounded, the same thing happened again in Nevada, only this time it was the transmission that was repaired but didn't have any fluid added. The book wasn't kind to the intellectual capabilities of auto mechanics. The result was a lot of time spent in garage waiting rooms, and the stories grew longer and richer.

Could someone else have heard the stories and written the book? The thought had Madeline flushed with excitement. Maybe Madeline and her mother had shared a waiting room or a campsite with Anne Shannon. Maybe Anne had listened to the stories, found them interesting, and decided to write them down, then published them. Yes, that was possible. Madeline thought about it, her adrenaline rising. She was becoming sure it was more than possible; it was the best solution to the mystery she had ever come up with. She could hardly wait to tell Steven and see what he thought. It could all make sense, it could all work out.

But why then would Anne Shannon work so hard to keep the origins of the book a secret? That was still strange.

The sun was gone. The western sky was like a pale lavender lace, and just when she began to wonder what had become of Steven, he slid two trays of food onto the deck and climbed up.

Madeline rose to meet him. She found herself in the comfortable haven of his arms. "What's this?" she asked timidly, drawing back, but feeling good, and a little giddy. The idea of Anne not being her mother didn't bother her at all.

"Well, if we are cousins, it's just a cousinly kind of a hug." The easy smile was back in his voice.

"And if we are not?"

"Then it's not at all cousinly."

"I see."

Steven laughed. "Is it that horrible?"

"No, of course not. I just don't know whether to be cousinly or not. I'm still a little confused, but I think I may have figured it out." She rushed to explain about the specks of dust and the waiting rooms, the stories and the people listening—maybe Anne listening, maybe Anne was there at the Hiking Viking. "It is possible, isn't it, Steven?"

"Of course," he agreed enthusiastically. "In fact it sort of fits with what my mother said."

Finally, Madeline took the lid off of her tray. She was ravenous and it smelled good.

"Leftovers, I'm afraid."

Indeed it was a blend of leftover vegetables and chunks of meat, shellfish, and poultry, on a bed of rice with a fringe of tropical fruit, mostly mango. It was delicious: each mouthful was delightful and different.

Steven went on. "According to my mother, Anne having a grown daughter would be a surprise—but not a complete shock. And if so, she wants to welcome you to the family. She says Auntie Anne was the stereotypical hippie—at Woodstock even. The family practically never heard from her for a few years. She lived in the interior bush of British Columbia, homesteading in a log cabin, and she joined a commune in Alberta, and worked in New York City, and spent a lot of time in California. To support herself she picked up odd jobs as she wandered about, but her goal always was to be a writer. She wrote stacks of poetry and occasionally little bits got published. So it's certainly possible she met you and your mother somewhere during her travels, and it is possible she wrote down the stories.''

Madeline finished a wedge of ripe mango. "So why keep it all a secret? Why won't she talk about it?"

"I don't know." Steven shrugged. "She will. She will. We'll go see her tonight."

They ate in reflective silence until Madeline interrupted with her other bit of news. "Steven, someone was in here this afternoon."

Steven shrugged off her concern. "Lois probably came in to tidy up."

"No, I don't think so, and"—Madeline reached for her pad—"they made a copy of these notes. See?"

His laden fork stalled in midair and settled back onto the plate. He took her pad.

"I did the pencil shading." She watched him. "Had to be Anne, I think, but I don't know why she'd bother and I'm not sure what it means."

Steven nodded. "She does know where we keep the spare keys." He was reading through the notes.

"And the dog—the night before, he was in the cabin. I woke up in the dark and he was in the room by the bed."

"Raleigh?"

"Yes, at least I think so. I woke up and I heard a dog and smelled a dog, but I never saw him. I was scared. I didn't get the light on until after I heard the dog run away and the door bang shut."

"Are you sure?"

"Yes, I didn't dream it."

"No voices, no person?"

"Someone must have let him in. I had locked the door. Raleigh couldn't have opened it, or shut it behind him."

"No." Steven was shocked. "Why would someone do that?"

"I don't know, and it had to be Anne."

"Yes, but . . ." There was concern apparent in his face, and confusion. "Madeline, you should have told me."

"I know."

"I'm not letting you out of my sight again."

Madeline found that funny. She laughed as she said, "Well, we'll have to see about that."

He looked up and a moment later smiled, then, feeling self-conscious, glanced back at the notes. "She made a copy of your notes," he murmured slowly, thinking out loud. "The only reason I can think of is she didn't know these facts, and if she didn't know them, then she isn't your mother." He waited a moment, then flourished the papers in the air. "She isn't your mother. She can't be your mother; your mother wouldn't need to copy these notes, would she?"

Madeline agreed with a nod. "She isn't my mother,

Death and Deception

but still, why would she make a copy of the notes? For what use?"

"I don't know." He shrugged. "It's strange. Even if she isn't your mother, why would she copy your notes?" He saw the little wallet of Polaroids. "Let's see those pictures."

As he flipped through the pages, Madeline related the story behind each picture and how the incident appeared in the book.

His voice was deep and slow with concern. "These pictures correspond so exactly with the book it's eerie."

"I know."

"Even if Anne met your mother and heard the stories and decided to write the book, it's amazing it turned out so identical to your trip. You'd think she'd leave out something or embellish somewhere with one of her own experiences."

Were they back at square one?

Steven flipped back through the pictures. He stared at the picture of Madeline at the Grand Canyon. There was nothing special in it that she knew; it was just a simple picture of her near a railing at the lip of the canyon.

"Look at the woman beside you."

"It doesn't look like my mother. I think my mom was taking the picture."

"No, it's not your mom." He scanned back to previous pictures where the woman identified as Madeline's mom was. The two women were similar in many respects, yet distinctly different. "But this woman looks like she is in your picture, you see? She is beside you and posing."

"It's the Grand Canyon. People were probably taking pictures everywhere. She was probably posing for someone else."

"But the camera almost seems to frame both of you."

"Look at the other pictures. My mom wasn't much of a photographer, strictly point and click."

He skimmed through the little stack and stopped at the picture on Clearwater Beach. "Look at this. Could this be the same woman?" He pointed at a woman standing just behind where Madeline was playing in the sand.

It was hard to be certain. One was a grainy, overexposed beach picture of a woman in a big hat and a little bikini squinting in the bright sun; the other picture showed a woman in jeans and a jacket with long hair fluttering in the breeze.

"It could be, I guess. I've been looking at these pictures for so many years, I guess I just stopped noticing things."

"Maybe someone was traveling with you. At least part of the time."

"It's possible."

"Anne?"

"Maybe. Maybe she knew your mother."

"It's impossible to be certain. But why lie?"

Madeline shrugged; it was like she was afraid to risk being too happy. "I keep thinking there is still more to the story, some dreadful secret."

He raised a hand to the side of her face, his fingers curled loosely. The knuckles touched and trailed along the soft smooth crest of her cheek and jaw and chin. His eyes were sincere and caring. She loved him with all her heart. She couldn't imagine being prevented from loving him. He didn't speak; he didn't have to. His eyes revealed everything.

Happiness was there like a big red apple dangling before her and all she had to do was reach out and pluck it. She could taste it. And yet... She was still scared. Her experience was that things went wrong. Her experience was that she could count on no one but herself, and that if she didn't expect happiness, she couldn't be hurt too badly.

The fear in her eyes melted his heart and he became confused. He saw the fear but didn't quite understand what it said. "We'll find out," he murmured.

"I..." She wanted to explain, explain everything, but how do you explain things that you don't even understand? She was glad just holding his hands, and there was hope again. That was enough for now. Her fears ebbed, and hope swelled. This time things could work out. She allowed herself to almost believe it.

Slowly the sun disappeared.

It was blissfully quiet. A knock at the front door

seemed so out of place, they didn't even notice it, not until there was a second, louder knock. Steven stacked all the dishes on one tray as Madeline passed back into the cottage and across the kitchen. She stopped in the darkness. Anne Shannon was there waiting, her profile visible through the small window in the door.

Chapter Twelve

Anne stared away from the door until the door opened, then she looked straight and hard at Madeline. When she noticed Steven approaching from behind, she looked away, momentarily lost in the depths of her own thoughts. Then she jerked her head up abruptly and once again stared at Madeline.

"Come in," Madeline tentatively suggested.

Anne entered but did not speak. No one spoke. It was like no one knew how to get started.

What to say, what to ask?

Anne's eyes stole glimpses of Steven; obviously she had not expected him to be there. It was like she was reconsidering something.

"All Madeline wants is the truth," Steven announced in a determined but not harsh voice, "about the book, about who her mother is. She's entitled to that, don't you think?"

Anne nodded. She turned and walked away but only for a couple of steps. She stopped. She looked at Steven first, then found Madeline. Keeping calm, steady eyes upon Madeline, Anne spoke. "I wrote the book," she stammered at first, but slowly gathered strength as she continued, "about a trip I took with my daughter. I am your mother."

Madeline felt her knees begin to give way. This wasn't right. She felt like falling, but refused. She questioned her hearing. *Did she say she was my mother? Is this a nightmare?*

Steven took her hand. Anne had admitted being Madeline's mother, just as Madeline had finally given up the idea. She didn't want Anne; she wanted Steven.

The interlude had allowed Anne to resume her cold composure. "So, all you want is the truth?"

"Yes," Madeline whispered, "yes, the truth."

"Nothing more, and that will be the end of it."

"Yes."

"You'll leave me in peace."

Madeline had already begun to nod, when Anne demanded stonily, "You'll leave?"

Madeline stopped in mid-nod, and began to think. *She still, and only, wants me to leave. This woman only wants me to leave.* Madeline's head was spinning. *She's my mother, but she only wants me to leave. She must hate me. Why? What did I do?*

"Okay, I'll tell you everything." Anne stopped and looked around the little room as if making sure there was no one else, no else could hear. "I've been living a lie for so long. I am your mother." She cleared her throat and began to speak like she was a schoolgirl giving a memorized speech. "I don't know how much you know, so I'll tell you. Your father was an American draft evader. When he found out about your anticipated arrival he suddenly wanted to become a responsible member of society, so he turned himself in to the authorities. When he finished his stint in the Army we were going to become a proper little Establishment family and settle down and live in California.

"I needed a green card to work in the States while I waited for Paul, so I bought one, an entire new identity. I have no idea where it came from or how it was produced, but it worked and I became Pamela Sue Paige.

"Then he died but I decided to move to California anyway so I took the trip that was eventually detailed in the book. I took the trip with a three-year-old child, but not you; you are a full-grown woman. You took the trip with a loving young mother, but certainly not me; I am not a loving young mother. Those people are gone. They have all vanished from the face of the earth."

It was all as Madeline had once surmised, exactly as she had recorded it in her notes. But this cold, distant relating of facts was worse than her denying it.

She felt like she was crumbling on the inside. She had a mother, but not really; she had Steven, but only as a cousin. Again she had nothing. She was alone.

"The trip happened exactly as it was in the book, disaster after disaster. It was like the van had been cursed. Ultimately I became desperate. There were so many bills for all the repairs. I had several credit cards all at their limits, no job, no money, no husband, no home, and a young daughter, so Pamela Sue Paige drowned. I knew I could become Anne Shannon again; I'd be reborn debtless and free. But you were Madeline Paige; you didn't have another identity. It was impossible for you to come along. Besides, you were better off without me, and I can see now I was right about that. You've turned out very well."

Anne had given her a compliment but it was without any semblance of care. Madeline was reeling. She felt Steven's hand squeeze snug upon hers. He was trying to give her strength.

"That's enough. I've told you what you want to know, haven't I? And that's all I'm saying. Except, I am sorry. I have made mistakes, plenty of them. I know that. I wish I could go back and undo some of the things I've done, but I can't, can I? I know I've hurt you. But there just is no way to go back, is there? Is there?" A trembling vehemence stole into her voice; Anne struggled to push it away. "There is nothing we can do now about the past. And there is nothing between us, there never ever will be. It's too late."

Death and Deception

Anne Shannon moved calmly away. She paused and turned. "Now, you've promised to leave."

Madeline was fighting hard, trying not to crumple to the floor. That took all her energy; she didn't have the strength to respond in any way.

"Yes, I am your mother." Anne announced the fact again, again with the coldness and distaste and disinterest of someone confessing to having eaten the last piece of chocolate cake. The words "so what?" hung in the air unspoken. There was no hint of tenderness or compassion, certainly no desire for a warm embrace.

"I'm sorry. I realize this isn't turning out as you expected, but I really think it is best if I don't have any more to do with you. I have my reasons. Move on; forget about me. You certainly don't need me, so get on with your life."

Stunned, Steven and Madeline were incapable of speaking; they were incapable of thought.

Anne stared at them, waiting. "Okay then, if that is all understood." She noticed the way they stood together, shoulder to shoulder, hand squeezing hand. "I'm sorry," she muttered once more. This time she seemed to mean it; there was a spark of compassion in her voice. Then she turned and left quickly, not running but quickly, out the front door and down the steps.

Suddenly Steven raced out after her. "How can you be so cruel?" Anne ignored him. She kept walking, not turning, and quickening her gait, nearly stumbling in the dark.

Madeline waited, stupefied, then the tears overwhelmed her, and she began to gasp back huge wet sobs. Immediately Steven came back. He was beside her, great pain evident in his eyes as he took her in his arms. "Give her time. I don't understand it. . . . How can anyone be so cruel?"

"I've got to go," she said, standing.

"You can't, not like this."

"I can't stay. I can't, I don't want to." Madeline was shaking with frustration. "Why stay?" she yelled. "I've found out everything, everything there is to know. I promised I'd leave."

"But we are cousins now, family. I'm here for you."

"Cousins!" Madeline screamed. "I don't want to be your cousin." She was crying. No one had ever seen her cry before, and it only made matters worse. It only made her cry harder. "No, that's not true, but—"

"You can't leave now, not like this. Listen to me. I won't let you go like this. I won't let you."

"Please." There was pleading in her eyes. She couldn't look at him. "I just want to go. I want to go home, now." She knew how to deal with heartrending pain, but only if she was alone.

"Wait till the morning at least. Sleep. We'll talk

about it in the morning, and if you still want to leave, I'll drive you."

Madeline kept crying. She pushed him away.

Steven repeated, "Tomorrow, if you still want to leave, I'll drive you anywhere you want to go—the train station in town, the airport in Saint John, or Montreal, or New York. I'll drive you all the way back to San Jose, if you'll let me. Tomorrow. You can't leave now, not like this."

"Will you leave me alone now?" She turned away from him. "I want to be alone."

Somehow she managed to convince him. Reluctantly, he left.

After a while Madeline began to pack again. She was relieved to be alone and glad to have some work to do. Her eyes were dry, yet she still cried. Her coming here had been a terrible mistake. It had brought anguish to everyone—herself, Steven, and even her mother, Anne Shannon. She wished she had never found the book. She would leave as soon as she could.

All packed, she allowed herself a moment to collapse onto the bed, just a moment to catch her breath and clear her mind.

Chapter Thirteen

The light that filtered through the bedroom window was dull and dusky. Madeline lay there in the shadows, listening to the quiet, not knowing if she found the tranquillity soothing or irritating, yet she was content to allow her mind to wallow in its numbness. She'd fallen asleep and drifted far away from the sea and Smith's Cove, from Steven and Anne Shannon, and resisted coming back. It was like she had forgotten who she was, where she was, or just didn't care.

Did she care?

With an effort, Madeline lifted her head up into the darkness, refocusing her mind on the tasks at hand. She swung her legs over the side of the bed and stood. Opening the bedroom door and turning on the living room light, Madeline saw the kitchen clock and realized she had only slept for about an hour. It was going to be a long night. She wasn't going to stop until she was back home, in the shimmering summer heat of California. She was shivering. The nights were too cool here: it would be good to be hot again. The air in California was so hot and thin you could scarcely breathe; it could bake the trembling out of you.

Madeline washed her face with cold water. She brushed her teeth and hair. Her eyes were rimmed with red, but she didn't care. Pulling shut the zipper on her windbreaker, she took one last look around her little cottage, then began to hurry. If she lingered, she was afraid she'd soon be too weak to leave. She had to get away. Out the door she fled, and scrambled across the grass, fairly running along the path.

The night was gray and damp. The dew had already fallen upon the grass and the fog was building. It made the moonlight silver, and ghostly.

It wasn't fair, she knew, not to stop and say good-bye to Steven, but she didn't think she could without breaking down before him, and incurring the heavy look of sympathy in his eyes. She had already seen it, and it hurt. She told herself she would write him in a few days when she was home and this was all more like a bad dream and less real. Then she paused to wonder if this cowardice was something she had inherited from her mother.

One thing she knew she did have the courage to do was go and face Anne Shannon and say good-bye; she would say it just as fiercely as Anne Shannon had said, "Now, leave." Madeline wanted Anne to know that she was leaving, keeping up her end of the bargain. Tempted, at first, to throw it in the woman's face, Madeline tempered her anger as she walked. She couldn't allow herself to become consumed by bitterness. It was another cruel, callous, and unjustified punishment inflicted upon her, but she must overcome it. She couldn't allow this to ruin her life. Somehow Anne had weakened and given in; something had overwhelmed her and destroyed her life, her happiness. Perhaps Madeline couldn't save her mother. The thought hurt. It caught in her mind—she struggled with the guilt that she had somehow, however inadvertently, caused the ruination of her mother's life—but she would work and fight for her own chance at happiness.

In the book, Anne had been so young and gleeful, a cheerful person; Madeline could remember that much. Her mother smiled, always smiled, even if Madeline couldn't clearly remember any smiles, intuitively she was certain. Her mother was the character in the book, not the woman in the stone cottage. Even when the constant van breakdowns were ruining the trip and devastating their finances, Anne, or Pamela Sue Paige, accepted her fate with a smile and a quip—it was all in the book. She found the humor in any situation, but Anne Shannon only knew how to suffer.

How could they be the same person? How could anyone change that much?

Madeline wouldn't allow herself to hate Anne. Her head was spinning in a fierce whirlpool of emotions. She knew she mustn't allow herself to succumb to the same weakness. It was easy to become bitter and hateful; sometimes it was hard work to nurture joy and happiness.

The night was rapidly darkening, no stars were visible, the fuzzy white cocoon was tightening on the full moon, and even the dull glow was fading.

Her harried walk slowed as she approached her mother's. Her mother's: there was no longer any doubt. Her mother, the one who had borne her, and who once upon a time loved her so eloquently that she had written a best-selling and powerful book about it, a testament to their love. That was the mother Madeline would remember, and cling to. For all intents and purposes, it was best to consider her mother dead, drowned many years ago while taking a morning swim in the Pacific Ocean. No, she railed against herself, she could make some sort of peace with Anne Shannon. She would try, and keep trying. She would say good-bye, but every Christmas she'd send a card and on birthdays, and Mother's Day: plain and simple ones, signed with just her name, nothing more. And even if her mother just threw them in the fireplace and burned them unopened, Madeline would find some solace that she herself had tried her best, and she'd keep trying. She wouldn't give up. And she would send cards and letters to Steven. It would hurt at first, but gradually they could become friends and cousins. Maybe it would hurt a little forever, but that was okay. She wouldn't give in; she'd handle it somehow.

Madeline looked up from her reverie. Once again she was on the veranda of the cold stone cottage. She knocked. The building was dark and quiet. In the grass, crickets chirruped. There was no answer, no sound of creaking floors, no snarling face in the cut-glass window. Madeline found that strange. The woman who rarely went anywhere was not home. Perhaps she'd gone for a walk on the beach—in the dark? On the slippery rocks? That wasn't reasonable. She must have gone to the inn, or to see Lois, or maybe into town. It wasn't that late. She checked her watch: after ten.

Madeline was determined to get this over with. Walking around the cottage, she looked for lights and peered in windows. At the front veranda she climbed up and knocked again on the glass doors. She remembered Raleigh and wondered where he was. What would she do if he came bounding around the corner? Putting her hand on the door handle, she gave it a little tug and was surprised when it began to slide open. Madeline hovered in the doorway. Sticking her head inside, she called, "Ms. Shannon?" There was still no answer.

She stepped inside—after all, Anne had broken into

her cabin, broken in and copied the notes. "Ms. Shannon?" she called loudly. Again, no answer; again there was only quiet and darkness.

Obviously there was no one home. It was silly to continue looking. But still . . . she couldn't leave. She was drawn into the house. Where was the dog?

"Raleigh?" she whispered, hoping he wouldn't appear. And he didn't. Nothing stirred.

"Ms. Shannon, it's me, Madeline. I've just come to tell you I am leaving." The words sounded absurd as she spoke them. She was calling her mother Ms. Shannon, but what else could she call her? "Anne," she whispered. Sliding shut the door behind her, she then swept her hand along the wall until she found a light switch.

Where was the dog?

Something was strange; but nothing looked the least bit strange. Everything was clean and tidy. The only thing wrong was she was intruding into someone else's home. She should leave. She knew she should, but couldn't.

Madeline was in the dining room. To the left lay the kitchen, which she entered, turning on lights as she went. In the living room she saw thin red embers glowing in the fireplace. Burned pages? A book? She flipped on another lamp. Madeline went to the bottom of the stairs and called again. Then she went up slowly. The bed was made up neatly, with fresh flowers in a vase on the night table. Across the hall, the room Anne must have used as a study was so tidy it looked disused. There was an envelope and a few papers on the desk; she resisted the temptation to read them. Suddenly Madeline was feeling repulsed at her own nefarious behavior. She shouldn't be in here—the words had been echoing in her mind all along, but now had become so loud she couldn't ignore them. Abruptly she turned to leave.

Then she heard a scamper, and quiet whining.

Madeline hurried downstairs.

Through the glass doors she saw Raleigh waiting out on the deck. He was wet and glistened in the light streaming from the dining room. When he saw her he leaped up and pounced against the glass, causing the doors to shake, then the huge dog hunkered down like he was trying to shrink and began to whimper.

Madeline waited and stared. She tried being friendly. "Hi ya, Raleigh."

He wagged his tail.

"Remember me? 'Course you do." She didn't dare open the door. His paws were as big as her head; each claw was as long and thick as one of her fingers, and a lot sharper. With these weapons he could indeed seriously maul her in joyful, playful exuberance.

"He's a pussycat," Steven had said. *A pussycat the size of a pony,* Madeline thought. "He's a pussycat," she repeated, trying to persuade herself.

"He's a good boy," she enthused in her most honeyed voice. "He's just a little pussycat."

The dog was going wild, sitting and yet moving in every direction at once.

Madeline slid open the door a crack. He jumped up. "Down," she instructed.

He hugged the deck, his tail flogging back and forth with syncopated thuds.

Cautiously, she reached out her hand, showing him the open palm; then, moving very slowly, she patted him on the side of his huge neck. He was slick, wet and sticky.

Raleigh squirmed and whimpered.

He'd been in the sea; how else could he get wet? "Where's your master, boy? Where's Mama?" Madeline whispered nervously. "Gone out for a walk?" She edged one foot through the door. "In the dark," she added, realizing just how black a night it was becoming, the stars and moon tucked beyond the ever thickening blanket of fog. Again she recalled Steven saying how well trained Raleigh was. He never left the property, knew the property line as well as a surveyor. The day he had chased her, he had stopped at the top of the steps. Cautiously she reached out an open palm, then stroked the back of Raleigh's head. It was wet and salt-sticky. So how did he get himself wet if not in the sea? Of course, he might leave the property with his master, with Anne.

A thought was already germinating in Madeline's mind. It was absurd; she resisted it.

Out now on the front veranda, Madeline was alone

with the beast. She left the door open, available for a hasty retreat, just in case. The dog reared up and leaped into the air. But he made no movement toward her, then raced off into the darkness, merely to return a moment later, only to turn, scamper, and disappear once again.

Madeline set off after him, across the damp grass, to the rock ledge and the wooden steps. There he was, chasing tight circles in the dark. His big, gyrating body occupied the full breadth of the top step. Madeline stopped. "Go on, Raleigh, go on." The dog was not inclined to go further. She took a breath and, pushing his back away from her, she squeezed past. She walked down onto the rocks. There was a creamy white dimness high in the sky and a glow from the Shannon cottage, but other than that she could see absolutely nothing. She needed the dog's help.

Raleigh did not follow.

"Come on, Raleigh." She slapped her thighs. "Come on, boy."

He didn't come. Madeline moved further into the darkness, her ankles twisting on the slick rocks beneath her feet.

"Anne?" she called. "Anne, are you out here?"

There was no answer. Madeline could no longer see the dog at all, or the ledge. This was crazy, she thought. She needed the dog.

"Raleigh," she demanded in a loud shout. "Come."

Death and Deception

There was a scratching of claws and she knew he was still running circles on the steps. He'd been trained to stay on the property, but he was wet. He'd been in the water. But he wouldn't have sneaked away alone. He must have gone with Anne. That meant her mother was . . .

"Raleigh!" she yelled in her most authoritative voice. "Come!"

One more quick scratch and then there was the sound of the beast gamboling over the rocks. Madeline braced herself, bending down, half expecting him to bowl her over.

"Where is she?" she hissed as the dog approached.

He brushed by and headed to the water's edge. She heard him splash. Madeline followed until her feet were wet. The sea was black and cool. "Where is she?"

The dog was paw-deep in the water beside her. He came out to the edge, walked around, pacing back and forth, back and forth, never straying more than a couple of feet from the spot, sniffing at the water and the rocks, turning in circles. Then he plodded back in.

"Where is she, boy?" Madeline whispered, continuing to reject the thought dominating her mind. "Where is she, Raleigh?" There were lots of more plausible explanations than that one. Maybe Anne had slipped on the wet rocks, twisted her ankle, or banged her head. She could be lying somewhere nearby unconscious. Madeline walked deeper into the water.

The tide was going out. If Anne was out here in the water, then . . . Madeline was up to her knees, up to her waist. She stopped. The water swirled and burbled around her. This was crazy, absolutely crazy. She would not go any farther.

Raleigh began to bark. He was out beyond her and paddling hard, zigzagging, looking for something. She could hear the silvery splashes stretching away into the distance.

She took another step. Crazy! She stopped. She was wandering out into cold, deep water in pitch blackness. If Anne had fallen and hurt herself, then surely she'd be on the beach. The only way she'd be in the water was if . . . Madeline remembered the police report, now twenty years old.

The water was gently undulating, breathing, as if it were a live thing. She felt certain that her mother was out there, and leaving, and Madeline wouldn't let her die again. But it was madness to wander into deep, cold water at night, with the tide flowing out. She had no real proof her mother was in the water, and if she was, what were the chances she could find her? And even if she did, then what? Drag her back to shore?

Amid the dog's distant splashes there was a muffled shout. "Home, Raleigh, home!"

"Anne!" Madeline screamed. "Anne!"

There may have been an answer lost in the din of churning water. Madeline began to swim, no longer thinking of the water, or herself, or the darkness. A moment later she was face-to-face with Raleigh; forever obedient, he was chugging for shore. He swam around her once, unsure of what to do, then he was gone, heading for the cottage.

This was what her mother had pretended to do twenty years before. Madeline didn't try to figure it out; she knew her mother was out there in the water.

"Anne! Don't!"

There wasn't any answer.

Madeline swam into the darkness.

Chapter Fourteen

It was one of those black and quiet nights where two old friends were on a roll, sitting on the porch of the Harbourview Inn and nursing their drinks, feeling full of wit and wisdom. Their wives had enjoyed a leisurely dinner with them, then gone home, but the men had no inclination to follow. Steven didn't mind. They were local cottagers and he knew them, and reminiscing, scheming, and solving the world's problems was something they often did. Usually his father would pull up a chair and join them.

Steven looked in from time to time. He freshened their drinks as need be, then returned to the bright kitchen where he half listened to "Ideas, with Lister Sinclair" on the local CBC radio station while he puttered around the kitchen. The next day was going to be another busy one. He had chicken breasts marinating in lime juice, garlic, and ginger, and strawberry pies with fresh-picked berries ready for the oven, and croissants and muffins ready to bake in the morning. There were always things to do in the kitchen.

It was good that he was becoming an old hand at this, because as he measured, kneaded, and flattened out with the rolling pin, his attention was not at all on his work. Mostly he thought about Madeline, and his aunt, whose behavior was beyond his comprehension. What possible reason could she have for rejecting her own daughter? Maybe Steven could reason with her. Madeline wanted nothing. She was a daughter anyone would be proud to have.

When finally the two stragglers decided to call it a night and the dining porch was empty, Steven closed up the inn. Tired yet restless, he elected to wander down to Madeline's cottage. He wouldn't disturb her unless the lights were on.

The little cottage was dark and quiet. Desperately, he wanted to rap on her door and see if she was okay, but he resisted. Madeline was asleep, he reasoned, and as much as he wanted to see her he decided it would be selfish to wake her now. A good night's sleep would be very good for her. So he returned to the inn. Entering through the kitchen door, he found the phone ringing. It was his mother.

"Listen, I know it's late," she began immediately. "Have I wakened you?"

"No, I—"

"I've thought of something here."

Steven wasn't aware of what exactly she was speaking of. "How's Dad? What have you thought of?"

"Improving, I think; it's hard to get a doctor to say anything definitive, you know, but I think the worst is over. I spoke to him, and he was resting quite comfortably, though with all the drugs... But Steven, there is something not right about your Madeline's story."

"What?"

"Well, I've thought a great deal about it. To be honest, Anne's life has always fascinated me. As a kid sister I was more than a bit envious, you know—she was the fearless adventurer in the family, and I was the timid mouse, and I am far too nosy— Oh, I'm rambling away here. Listen, your grandmother Thorne died on August the eleventh, 1970, and we found Anne. She was living in New York and she came to the funeral looking rather haggard and melancholy; said she had a dull job and was working hard on her poetry. She stayed for a week, so we would have noticed, I mean—"

"Noticed what, Mom? I don't understand."

"Well, you see, she wasn't pregnant. According to what you told me, Madeline was born less than two weeks later. I think we would have noticed if Anne were nine months pregnant. So, obviously she isn't Madeline's mother."

"But Mom, Anne admitted being Madeline's mother."

"She did?"

"Yes, just this evening."

"She did?" Mrs. Raven repeated in astonishment. "Why? She couldn't be."

"Well, she did. Maybe someone has their dates wrong."

"Their date of birth wrong? I don't think so. And I'm absolutely certain when my mother died."

Steven shrugged. "I don't know, but this has Madeline very upset and she wants to leave immediately. I told her to wait until morning." Steven realized his eyes were suddenly wet. He was struggling to speak. He couldn't let her leave.

"Yes, of course it's upsetting her, the poor girl." Mrs. Raven could hear the tears in her son's voice. She knew exactly how he felt. "But Steven, listen to me, I know when my mother died. If Madeline was born on September first, 1970, then Anne couldn't possibly be Madeline's mother, can she?"

"But Anne said . . . Was she lying?"

"Stevie, I think she must have been lying for a long time."

"But why?"

Chapter Fifteen

The water was cold. And while the surface was almost mirrorlike, Madeline could feel she was moving, swept along by the current. In all directions there was only black, becoming a thick gauzy black as the fog seemed to intensify and lower down to touch the water. She tried to orient herself, reasoning that the river flow and tide would be sweeping her away from shore and swiftly out into vast Passamaquoddy Bay. Her mother had likely started from the same place on the beach, and probably was not bothering to swim, content to let the water pull her along. Therefore Anne should be just ahead and traveling in a similar direction. Madeline thought about sailing with Steven and the way the boat drifted with the current. If Madeline swam just a little, in the same direction as the flow, she should catch up to her mother. She didn't consider what she would do then, or how she could possibly find her way back to shore, any shore. First she had to find and grab hold of her mother. And this time she wouldn't let her go—not ever.

She swam as silently as she could, doing the breaststroke on the surface. A few strokes, then she coasted, listening, always thinking that maybe she heard something. There was an indistinct and tired whisper from the moving water, and she thought she could hear an eerie moan, but no sound of movement, no indication anyone, or anything, was in the water nearby.

The corduroy slacks Madeline wore, the blouse, light jacket, and sneakers were encumbrances, but they offered some warmth, and she didn't want to swim too fast; she wanted to catch Anne, not pass her in the dark. Already the chill had seeped deeper into her body; she could feel it, or rather, she could feel the numbness. Her skin was thick and felt rubbery, her fingers nonexistent, but her knees ached—was that a good sign or bad? How long could someone survive in this cold water? The question wandered in and out of the dark recesses of her mind and she kept trying to push it back there as far as she could. It was too late to turn around anyway, she reasoned. She doubted she could swim against the current even if she tried, even if she knew which way to go. It was best to keep warm by moving and swimming a little. Consciously she thought only of finding her mother.

She knew her mother was out here—somewhere. It was crazy but she knew she could catch her, at least she was certain she had to try. How many times had she thought about saving her mother that night twenty years ago, when she was only five? Of course, she couldn't have then, she was only a child, asleep and unaware, but that was no solace. This time her mother was nearby, very near, and to do something so desperate, she must be suffering horrible mental anguish.

Madeline hung motionless in the water. There was a faint gurgle.

Madeline cried out, "Anne!" She waited for an answer, then dug into the water. She swam hard for several strokes, then waited. "Anne?" she whispered.

Steven waited impatiently. He knocked again on the cabin door, louder this time. Something was wrong. Why wasn't she answering the door? He called again. He couldn't wait for morning. Madeline would want to know this right away. He pounded hard, then took out the key.

Could his mother be somehow wrong? Surely she would have noticed if her sister were nine months pregnant. Could Madeline's date of birth be wrong? Why?

The door caught and he had to shove it open.

"Madeline!" She wasn't here. He knew it immediately. He turned on lights. All her belongings were gone. She'd already left. She'd already left for home. He had to catch her.

Chapter Sixteen

Anne was near, so near Madeline could hear the water curl around the body, she could hear the labored breathing. Where?

"Anne! Anne, please."

A muffled voice choked, "Leave. Leave me alone." The voice was lost in the black, but Madeline thought it was to the right and close, very close.

"Mother," Madeline gasped, reaching out.

"No!" came back a scream. There were frantic splashes.

Madeline charged forward once more, grasping into the darkness, catching black water and more water and something hard. A foot? She was certain it was a foot in a shoe, but it broke away from her grasp. Madeline swam again, grabbing a leg, and pulling fabric and snaring a belt loop which gave a secure hold.

Anne struggled. "No! No!" she screamed hysterically. "Why didn't you just leave? Why can't you? Haven't you done enough? You've ruined everything! Go back—go!" She gave another angry twist and tried to pull away, flailing with her arms, splashing and kicking.

Madeline held firm. She didn't know what else to do. She waited, her legs slowly bicycling in the cold water.

Anne continued to fight and cry until gradually she gave up and fell limp and lost in weak sobs.

Madeline came behind the older woman and caught her up with her arms and held her snug. Anne allowed herself to be held, allowed her head to slump down upon Madeline's shoulder. They were swept along with the current. They were quiet.

Finally Anne spoke. "It's not true," she admitted with weakness and pain.

"What?" Madeline asked.

"Everything. It's my fault, all of it. *I* ruined everything, not you. I don't deserve to live." Anne gave a halfhearted wrench, almost twisting away.

"Don't say that." Madeline reasserted her grip. She wouldn't let go.

"Just leave me. It's okay. It's for the best. Everything will be better with me gone. Just go back to shore." Anne began again to squirm. "Go. Go back."

"I can't. I'm not going to leave you."

"Let me go." She was crying and swimming and fighting at the same time. "Leave me, leave me. Don't you understand? I don't want you here."

That was something Madeline understood very clearly. Anne didn't want her. "Why, why do you hate me so much?"

Anne was gasping, and the words came out in fierce little bursts. "I don't hate you. I don't even know you."

"You are my mother."

"No. You still think that? I couldn't possibly deserve you. I'm really not . . . your mother."

"Don't say that."

"I've lied so much. Even when I told the truth it was a lie. . . ." Anne almost laughed; it was more like a dry snicker. "It's hard to know anymore."

Madeline waited. She sensed a denouement, the opportunity for forgiveness and the chance for reconciliation. It seemed more important than life itself.

"Go back to shore. Please. Quick, before it's too late. I don't want you to die too."

Madeline listened to her mother shivering with cold. "We'll go together. It's not too late."

"Leave me, leave me. It's better this way, really. This is what I want."

"It's not what I want."

Anne was racked with sobbing. "I've ruined your life. And now . . . this. You should let me go, just let me go. Trust me, it's best." She began again to wiggle and squirm.

Madeline moved to face the woman. She had a hand on each hip, each thumb secure in a belt loop.

"To have . . . a daughter . . . like you, your mother must . . . have been very special."

Why was she saying this?

"I wish, I wish . . . you were my daughter. I wish I was the one who wrote that book."

Madeline wondered if the woman was delirious. The cold was strengthening its icy grip. Was she losing consciousness? What was she saying? Why was she saying that?

Anne had fallen to mumbling. Then she fell silent and limp.

"Anne?" Madeline called, and shook the woman gently. "Anne?" Anne's head toppled from side to side as Madeline shook her harder and harder. Finally Madeline just screamed for help, knowing she had gone too far; the mist would muffle the sound. No one would hear. Still she waited quietly, hoping for an answer, then she leaned back in the water, drifting, holding her mother in front, with one arm stretched across the older woman's thin chest, the other hand slowly sculling to maintain stability.

The current seemed to be easing. She didn't know if it was because they were out in deeper, wider water, or if the tide was slackening; she suspected it was both. When the tide reversed, she wondered, would it sweep them back ashore? No. It would help, but that was all. The river current combined with the ebb tide, she realized, remembering the afternoon spent sailing with Steven. But when the tide began to rise, the river would fight against it.

She shivered, feeling thin with the cold. Her feet resisted moving. She tried to kick but couldn't feel the slosh of the water against her skin. She had no idea anymore which way to swim. No sense of tide or any motion. She was drifting. No idea what to do. *Perhaps in a while the tide will change,* she thought, *but we'll never last that long.* Already Anne felt icy to the touch. But her teeth still chattered, so she was alive, if only semiconscious.

The sporadic moan of a deep, dull horn became gradually louder. She listened to it, trying to concentrate, at first thinking it was a boat, but numbly realizing it was only a fog buoy. She remembered the red buoy in the bay; there were others marking the channel. Should she try to find the channel, hoping to meet a boat? There'd be no boats out at night, not in this fog, and it wouldn't see them regardless; more likely a boat would just run them down. Or should she swim away from the channel, hoping to chance upon land, or an island? But she didn't know where anything was, so it didn't much matter, did it?

If only the sun would rise. What time could it be?

She closed her eyes to rest them, and drifted. Her mother began to slip from her grasp and she flailed like in a dream, and woke, and caught hold once more, clenching tightly. "Mom," she whispered. The woman groaned, and that was a relief. She was determined not to let her go.

She would never let her go.

Steven used Anne's phone. He was furious with himself for having wasted so much time. From the inn he had phoned the taxi company and the bus and train station. He'd phoned the police. Everyone knew him and was eager to help, but no, they hadn't seen a young woman traveling alone, and yes, they'd keep an eye out for her and give her his urgent message. They'd call him.

Then Steven got in the inn's little pickup truck and swiftly cruised the local roads, hoping to see her walking. She'd vanished. He thought to try her cottage again, then on a hunch he decided to try Anne's. Why hadn't he thought of her sooner?

Anne's cottage was lit up like a party was in progress. But no one was there, only Raleigh in the shed that was his doghouse. Steven had run through the building. On the desk in the upstairs study he had found the note, then Madeline's knapsack on the front veranda by the open sliding glass door. It took a moment, but he figured out what had happened. Raleigh eagerly led him to the beach. Steven had screamed her name. He had started to kick off his shoes, but he knew too much time had passed; he couldn't catch them by swimming. He had to think of another way.

"Look, Andrew," he repeated, trying to remain calm, "there really are two people lost out in the bay. No, they are in the water. No, it didn't sink; there wasn't a boat. Listen, it's not really important why they are in the water; they are, I know they are."

On the desk he had sketched an outline of the river and the bay.

"Hey, I know they won't last long." His voice rose; his patience was wearing thin. "That's why we have to hurry. I need to use your boat. We have to get every boat we can out into the water looking."

He guessed at a time and added a line to his drawing. He knew the strength and direction of the current.

"We can't possibly wait for morning. Just trust me, Andrew. Give me your boat!"

Chapter Seventeen

With *Toots warm in my arms even the coldest desert nights were only cool around the edges.*

"Only cool around the edges." Madeline's blue lips moved to repeat the words but made no sound. *". . . warm in my arms."*

We'd been in tight spots before, so when the van like some ornery beast decided it no longer wanted to go up the big mountain (I had the pedal to the metal; the motor was racing) and instead wanted to try capering backward along the edge of twisty cliffs and serious rocks, I only panicked for as long as it took to see Toots, then I smiled. Here we go again.

Madeline saw the words on the page. Gradually she envisioned her mom's smile.

I plucked up Toots in my arms, broke out of the van, and ran for dear life....

"... *in my arms, in my arms,*" Madeline repeated to herself.

Something shoved against her numb foot—she sensed it first vaguely in her hip—a rhythmic pushing, pausing and pushing again, a pressure on her hip as her leg was forced to pivot. But it wasn't enough to disturb her reverie.

He took out a pair of scissors and cut the plastic card into tiny pieces. I didn't crumble like I thought I might. Thank goodness I had my Toots in my arms. I was still the richest woman in the world.

Counting out the little stack of fives and tens, I had to hold Toots. This was it; we were down to nickels. I left the counter and caught her on a bounce and swung her up onto my hip, hugged her tight in my arms, too tight maybe, then kissed her, and laughed. We were together. Who could ask for anything more?

Something was rubbing against her leg. Then Madeline felt something grating on her. She woke and recoiled away, flailing her legs in sudden terror, splashing, and reaching down, pushing away with her free hand. There was something there. Solid. Slippery. Land? She hadn't thought it could be land. Land! She fumbled to get her legs under. It was land. Flush with relief, Madeline squatted, rising up out of the water, before a surge of water pushed her down. Grabbing Anne under the arms, she struggled to drag her up. She slipped and stumbled, sensation slowly came back into her numb and clumsy feet. The commotion caused Anne to stir, and groan out a complaint.

The water became shallower. With a sense of hope burgeoning, Madeline kept fighting. She almost had Anne completely out of the water, pulling her onto the smooth rock. One great effort and she dragged Anne another couple of feet and collapsed.

Between the plaintive moans of the foghorn she could hear Anne breathing and the subtle play of the water as it nibbled at the edge of the rock. Where were they?

She huddled up snugly against Anne, and tried to share warmth. Whether she slept or not, or just blacked out for a moment, she couldn't be sure, but when she opened her eyes it was still black and cold. She shivered in her wet clothes but it was not as paralyzingly cold as the water had been.

She tried to see. Stretching wide her eyes and staring was futile. All was blackness save a faint glimmer issuing from the water.

Madeline could feel the weak rise and fall of Anne's chest. She stumbled to her feet. She hadn't the strength to take Anne with her, and she couldn't leave her long here, wherever they were. The tide would rise once again and she'd be swept away. If she just knew which direction to drag her and how far it was to safety, maybe then she could do it. She was afraid, though, that if she set out, she'd never find her mother again.

I'll take ten straight steps, and only ten steps in one direction. Maybe I can find something. Taking only seven steps, Madeline found the rocks were slipping back beneath the water. She was hip deep. After returning to Anne, Madeline swung ninety degrees and managed only four steps, before slipping on a steep, slick rock and sliding over the edge, plunging deep. She flailed back to the surface, gasping, icy terror freezing her screams inside her. She caught the rock and scratched back out, then lay panting, trying to quell the still-surging panic. To calm her frayed nerves, she quickly got to her feet and cautiously tried the last direction. It seemed promising. Seven, eight, nine slow small steps, she felt like she was rising, but the tenth sank down. She carried on—eleven, twelve, thirteen, her ankles were wet. Fifteen, sixteen, she was knee deep in cold water.

It was a mere rock ledge she had discovered. No more than a tabletop in the water, a table that very soon would hide back deep beneath the incoming tide, the fifteen-foot tides. She went back to Anne. Finding her was easy; the tabletop was small.

In the distance the foghorn kept up its low moaning,

pausing, then moaning again. Madeline was exhausted when she sank down beside Anne, shivering and hoping to share some warmth. But Anne was awake and sitting up. "Where are we?"

Madeline washed the distress from her voice.

"A little beach."

"Shore?"

"Just a little island."

Anne thought about this a long time. "I'm cold," she muttered, and Madeline wiggled closer, sitting behind and hugging; then dissatisfied, she lifted the older woman into her lap like she was cradling a baby. "You should have let me go," Anne muttered.

Madeline protested, "No."

"Once again I've ruined your life. You should be safe, asleep, in your own bed. You should be in California, warm... Now, thanks to me, you will never be warm again."

"Don't be silly."

"But I'll be warm," Anne started perversely, "where *I'm* going. Soon." Then she began to chortle and ended racked with coughing.

It took Madeline a moment to realize what the woman meant. "No," she countered. "Why do you say that?"

Anne swallowed and waited. "I've lived here a long time. I know what you mean by a small island, and I know where I'm going when I die. I made my deal with Lucifer long ago. Not a very good deal either, but I wanted it so very badly."

Madeline was speechless.

"You still don't know, do you? You don't know what I've done. Done to you. Done to myself. Everything . . . it seems . . ." Her voice trailed off and Madeline wondered if Anne was losing consciousness. "I deserve this."

"No."

"You above all people should say good riddance. I am not your mother. I *stole* your mother, I stole your birthright." The woman was rambling, dreamlike. She sounded delirious, and yet she somehow sounded more lucid than ever.

"You, Madeline are precious and good, too good. You should never have come after me. I ruined your life. I didn't think you would ever know; I convinced myself you wouldn't, you were too young. I thought it was a shame about your mother, but you'd be okay. I didn't know all the evil I would cause you. You should never have tried to save me." Her voice was slow and deep. "I'm sorry."

It was taking all of Madeline's energy to stop from crying. In a strange way, she was crying partly from happiness. She was finally feeling close to her mother. Intuitively she knew she was getting closer to the truth.

Then Anne Shannon muttered, "If I had a daughter, I could only wish she was as nice as you."

Death and Deception

Madeline was tossed into confusion.

"I'm not your mother," Anne said. "I'm Anne Shannon; I was always Anne Shannon. I never took on a false identity, or married or had a child."

"But..."

"Listen to me. I'm a horrible person. I didn't mean to be. I'm not your mother. I never knew her, but I think she must have been a wonderful person. She had a wonderful daughter, and wrote a wonderful book. I'm afraid she must have died like they said." Wonderment crept into Anne's voice. "Maybe something like this, but I don't think so. I think your mother was like you. She'd never give up." In the eerie silence that followed, her teeth succumbed to chattering.

"I'll tell you everything. Everyone will know soon enough, so you should know. It would be cruel irony if, after all this, you died thinking I was really your mother, if you died not knowing the simple truth. I left a letter on my desk addressed to you, anyway. Someone will find it. The world will know soon enough, but you should know before—"

Anne's body convulsed like she was trying to get away, but she wasn't. She fell silent, and Madeline thought she might have lost her. Then Anne began to ramble in a low, weak, and garbled voice. She was expending precious energy to speak.

"It's okay. Don't talk," Madeline said. "Rest."

Anne ignored her. "You spoiled everything. For years I was afraid of you—not that it's your fault, I guess. I'm the villain. I always wanted to be a writer. I wanted it so bad I made my deal—" She started to cough, but struggled to keep speaking. "I . . . I . . . I was a wild child, living everywhere, doing everything. I called it researching life." She gulped, paused, then her voice rose precipitously. "I had to live, I had to research life, so I could write the great books. And I lived, and wrote and wrote and wrote, terrible pompous stuff, poetry mostly—trash, all horrible trash. But at the time, I thought they were great."

She wanted desperately to confess but still she was avoiding telling Madeline the ultimate truth, speaking only to build up confidence.

"It's okay to hate me," she mumbled.

"I don't hate you. I've never hated you."

"You will. You see, to make money before I achieved fame and fortune as a writer, I was a reader for Evergreen Press, a tiny publishing house—alternative stuff, you know, long gone now. And one day I read a manuscript that I thought was truly inspired, pure magic. I wanted to show it to my boss, but as luck would have it, he'd left early for a long weekend. I decided to phone the author. That's when I found out the author, your mother, had disappeared and was presumed drowned." In fatigue and sorrow her voice weakened. "Between the time she mailed us her manuscript and the time I finally read it she had drowned. She really did drown, I'm afraid, Madeline, long ago. I'm sorry."

Madeline bit the inside of her cheek. She didn't know what to think.

"I thought about that manuscript over the weekend, and for weeks afterward. I kept it and never told anyone I had it. Somehow, I thought if I could put my name on it, and get it published, it would help me with my own writing career. I'd have a little money, and time to write, and publishers would know my name and be eager to publish my other works. Your mother was dead; I couldn't see what harm there would be. I wanted to be a writer so... desperately. I loved books. I still love books. So I changed a few details, very few, because every time I tried to change a name, or anything, the story lost a little something. I couldn't even alter a name without harming her masterpiece. Two years I waited before I submitted it, just to be safe, just in case your mother had sent copies somewhere else as well.

"Well, I never dreamed it would catch on the way it did—just one of those inexplicable things that happen sometimes in publishing. It was good, very good, but it touched a nerve. Next thing I knew I was a little bit rich and a little bit famous. People thought I was a genius, but your mother was the genius. They came from all over the country to ask me questions, questions that I really couldn't answer. Like about J J—I kept expecting someone to dig up the real J J and have a reunion with me and have the truth come out. So I became a recluse and came here to hide and work on my 'second' book. But..."

Madeline was aware the tide was beginning to rise up the rock. The water was colder than ever.

"Then *you* came. I couldn't get rid of you. I told you I didn't know anything about you. I tried just not talking, but I guess you wanted a mother as badly as I had once wanted to be a writer. I saw your notebook, so I told you what I thought you wanted to hear. I thought you'd leave. Then I saw you and Steven together and—" Anne suddenly convulsed; her body shook like it had been hit with an electrical charge. Madeline struggled to maintain her grip. Then, as Anne finally settled still, she began to mumble, "I wish... I wish I'd never seen that book. As much as I love that book, I hate it."

The foghorn kept up a dull and distant moaning.

"Maybe... maybe, if I hadn't... Maybe, I could have written... I wish I could have written my own... any... I love books." Her last words were just a faint and distant whisper.

Madeline realized Anne was slipping back into unconsciousness. She gave her a shake. "Anne," she whispered.

Anne mumbled, "I'm sorry." And it sounded so faint and final that Madeline screamed, "Anne!" and shook her hard but it was no use. Anne could no longer respond. She was still alive; Madeline was sure of that because Anne still shivered, but slowly the

Death and Deception

shivering stopped too. At first Madeline thought Anne had slipped away entirely, but the frail, cold wrist still seemed to have the weakest of pulses, so irregular that it was hard to be certain. Madeline hugged the body tightly, massaging the surface, trying to create friction and warmth. She had no idea what time it was but surely the sun would be up soon. It had to be.

As the tide rose Madeline pulled the body to the highest surface on the rock, but even there the water was soon lapping around their legs. She lifted Anne up higher. She knew she didn't have the strength to stand and hold her. Slowly she began floating and drifting again. It was hopeless. She set off with the current hoping it would bring her back to shore, knowing she couldn't possibly make it.

If only the sun would rise, and the fog would clear, maybe then ... maybe there was a bigger island nearby. She thought of the big empty bay she had sailed on with Steven and the rocks and buoys. She thought of Steven.

Her mind was slipping. For warmth she thought of Steven, who wasn't her cousin, who had never been her cousin. If only she wasn't so cold.

Anne no longer shivered. It had been a long time since she had spoken, a long time since she had moved. The goose bumps had flattened away out of her skin. If there was a pulse or respiration Madeline couldn't feel it. She couldn't detect any signs of life at all, but still she held her tight. The thought of letting go never occurred to her—few controlled thoughts occurred.

Her mind had begun to float, much like her body was. She herself was no longer shivering. In fact she felt sort of warm and happy, and sometimes she saw lights, but she knew her eyes were closed and she knew she was sort of sleeping. To keep warm Madeline kept thinking of Steven. Sometimes he was there and so close she could hear his gentle voice. "Thank goodness you're early." He was smiling; he was laughing. "Try your best, that's all, that's the important thing." He was always smiling, always smiling, and she was sleeping, sleeping in her warm cozy bed with the flannel sheets—she loved flannel sheets, she never knew she loved flannel sheets, squeaky wood floors, and antique wood furniture, with clear stain so you could trace the grain of the wood. And flannel sheets and big feather pillows were wonderful. She'd never had flannel sheets before . . . and heavy blankets . . . and duvets, and big fat feather pillows, and scallops and red wine. . . . She could sleep forever. She was so cozy, in such a deep delicious sleep.

Except now they were yanking at her—someone was, and that wasn't nice. She wanted to sleep, and she was sleeping, she was determined to go right on sleeping, and dreaming. She was so tired, she felt like she was rising up, floating into the air, into the clouds. Then she started to fall and couldn't stop.

Chapter Eighteen

Her eyes wouldn't wake up. Already her ears did; she heard but didn't understand. There were murmurs, concerned voices speaking, mentioning her name. She wanted to open her eyes, but oh, those flannel sheets were so cozy and warm, deliciously warm, and the pillows so incredibly deep and soft.

Steven? She tried to open her eyes. That was his voice. That was his hand on hers. She wanted to see his smile, his eyes, and she did. Even with her eyes closed she could see him. She could hear his voice so clearly it was like he was there beside her. She knew if she opened her eyes that he'd be gone. Awaken, and the dream would be lost.

She smelled croissants and coffee. Madeline stretched long in the crisp flannel. Her fingers and toes fairly burned with warmth. Her mouth was dry and her stomach growled. Croissants. Her mind added bacon, and eggs in those little eggcups.

That was Steven speaking, and others. She didn't understand what they were saying.

Desperately she kept trying to open her eyes, till finally her lids parted, revealing a crowd of people in a small room—many, many people staring at her, starting to smile; they were starting to smile. She was in a bed, with heaped blankets and flowers on the nightstand. Where was Steven? She turned her head. He was standing beside her. He was holding her hand and trying to smile but he was crying. He was happy, and so was she, and they began to cry together. Neither could stop.

Epilogue

There was never any question where the wedding would be.

The tiny chapel overflowed, as usual. And again more tables and chairs had to be borrowed for the reception, which spilled out of the dining porches and into the lobby. The menu featured fresh smoked scallops embellished with peaches, a new Harbourview tradition, and white wine dyed red, in honor of the bride.

But these things were not terribly important. For this wedding, Steven and Madeline agreed the most important thing was that everyone could attend: Steven and Madeline, of course; and Steven's mother and father, of course; and his sisters, and all the locals and all the cottagers too. Everyone was there and that was the important thing. Even Steven's aunt came, Anne Shannon. She was reluctant at first, but she knew better than to try to thwart Stevie, or Madeline.